A Candlelight Ecstasy Romance®

"GO FIND ANOTHER DUMB, NAIVE WOMAN. WHILE YOU WERE GONE, THIS ONE GREW UP."

Mark grabbed her wrists to keep her from leaving the room. The gamble he'd taken by returning was doomed to failure unless he played his wild card. "Can you honestly say you don't love me?"

"Yes!" Sara answered vehemently.

"Then say it." He let go of her hands. "Say it, sweetheart, mean it, and I'll leave. You'll never see me or hear from me again."

The thought of him keeping that promise drained her anger, leaving Sara weak. It wasn't an idle threat. "I don't . . ."

"Say it all. Say, 'Mark, I don't love you.'" Mark's eyes blazed with pain.

She struggled, unable to repeat the five simple words.

CANDLELIGHT ECSTASY ROMANCES®

TEARS OF LOVE

Anna Hudson

Copyright © 1984 by Anna Hudson

All rights reserved. No part of this book may be reproduced or transmitted in any form or by any means, electronic or mechanical, including photocopying, recording or by any information storage and retrieval system, without the written permission of the Publisher, except where permitted by law.

Dell ® TM 681510, Dell Publishing Co., Inc.

Candlelight Ecstasy Romance ®, 1,230,851, is a registered trademark of Dell Publishing Co., Inc., New York, New York.

ISBN: 0-440-18634-X

Printed in the United States of America

June 1984

10 9 8 7 6 5 4 3 2 1

WFH

A CANDLELIGHT ECSTASY ROMANCE®

Published by
Dell Publishing Co., Inc.
1 Dag Hammarskjold Plaza
New York, New York 10017

Dedicated to: Rita Gallagher, my mentor, my friend. This
"feather" is special for both of us.

Dell ® TM 681510, Dell Publishing Co., Inc.

Candlelight Ecstasy Romance®, 1,203,540, is a registered
trademark of Dell Publishing Co., Inc., New York, New York.

ISBN: 0-440-18634-X

Printed in the United States of America

June 1986

10 9 8 7 6 5 4 3 2 1

WFH

To Our Readers:

We have been delighted with your enthusiastic response to Candlelight Ecstasy Romances®, and we thank you for the interest you have shown in this exciting series.

In the upcoming months we will continue to present the distinctive sensuous love stories you have come to expect only from Ecstasy. We look forward to bringing you many more books from your favorite authors and also the very finest work from new authors of contemporary romantic fiction.

As always, we are striving to present the unique, absorbing love stories that you enjoy most—books that are more than ordinary romance. Your suggestions and comments are always welcome. Please write to us at the address below.

Sincerely,

The Editors
Candlelight Romances
1 Dag Hammarskjold Plaza
New York, New York 10017

TEARS OF LOVE

PROLOGUE

She stood rigid and alone under the dimly lit streetlight. Sara Manchester dreaded the parting river mist. The nightmare was a heartbeat away. Sara couldn't hold back the haunting images. The scars on her soul couldn't be denied.

Winter's snow covered the long, parallel skid marks on the pavement. But she could see them. Her eyes narrowed as she tried in vain to see the drunk driver who had careened from the street, jumped the curb, and hit Sara and Mark's four-year-old son, Jamie.

Her mind's eye envisioned the cold chrome smashing her reason for living. Sara covered her ears. Had that heart-wrenching sound come from her—or had it come from her dying son? No one could answer the questions. There were no other witnesses to the fatal accident. Only Sara saw the car jerk backward, shudder as though shaking off responsibility for the heinous crime, and swerve back onto the street.

"Mommie! It hurts."

It hurts. Her shoulders slumped further as she wrapped her arms around her chest. Her gloved hands clutched the coat collar closer. The cold mist seemed to penetrate to her bones. Did the hurting ever stop? Her pain increased as she relived watching the ambulance driver wrap a white sheet around the small, broken body of her son. Jamie's pain had ceased; hers intensified. She had silently screamed in agony as she had chosen the garments and the coffin in which to bury her son. The anguish became tenfold as friends had gathered, offering condolences. When did the hurting stop?

"Never," Sara mumbled fatalistically.

The car should have hit her, she thought guiltily for the thousandth time. Why not her? Why him? He'd barely lived. Oh, God, she silently pleaded, why Jamie? She would gladly have given her life to spare her son.

Life was unfair. Death shouldn't strike the young. She had made so many mistakes in her twenty-seven years but none of this magnitude. She blamed herself for not seeing the car, for not hurling herself in its path . . . for living while her son died.

Wrapped in a depression darker than her coat, she turned from the site of the horror and trudged up Kingshighway Street, past St. Joseph's Hospital, on to her restored, turn-of-the-century St. Charles, Missouri, home.

Sara Manchester was unaware of the icy tears slipping down her hollowed cheeks; some dripping silently onto her serviceable dark coat, others shimmering on her chapped lips. Tears, nature's antiseptic, were washing the psychological wounds. Numbness had protected her sanity for the past few weeks. Until this moment she had been unable to cry.

Fumbling in her pocket, Sara's hand withdrew the large, old-fashioned key and inserted it into the lock. Warmth and silence greeted her. Closing the door, removing her coat, she glanced at the mahogany coatrack. Its empty hooks reinforced her loneliness. She touched the hook that had once held Mark's brown work jacket. Her hand slid along the highly polished surface to the brass hook that had held Jamie's assortment of jackets. Sara groaned as she placed her coat on "Mom's hook."

It was the little everyday happenings, inconsequential in the past, that haunted Sara now.

She mechanically climbed the worn hardwood steps, then went down the hall past Jamie's room and on to the master suite. She didn't stop by Jamie's room and stare as she often did. She couldn't.

Mentally exhausted, she undressed in darkness. She draped her suit jacket, ivory blouse, brown woolen skirt, and underwear over a maple rocking chair. Too weary to slip on a nightgown,

11

she eased her naked body between the cool, scented sheets. She reached for the adjoining pillow. It, like the hook downstairs, was empty. She longed for Mark.

CHAPTER ONE

Rapping on the glass inscribed, Dr. Jared Bishop, Counselor, Sara cracked open the school psychiatrist's door. Her eyes sought the welcoming smile of her colleague and friend.

"Come in, Sara," Jared said in a soft Southern drawl. "Beth Ann asked about you yesterday. How's the district's finest English teacher on this beautiful spring day?" Jared made a quick assessment of her appearance. Slender, blond, and dark-eyed, Sara was meticulously groomed in a navy blue suit, but the vibrancy usually surrounding her was missing. His relaxed form became alert as he extended his open hands across the green pad covering his desk. "Problems?"

"Thanks for seeing me after school," Sara said, avoiding his question. She placed her hands in his, slightly squeezing them before sitting on the edge of the leather chair near his desk.

"So how's it going?" Jared asked conversationally, running his hand through his dark hair, which was lightly peppered with gray.

"I'd like to say better, but I won't waste your time with a lie." Sara heard his squeaking chair and watched Jared straighten and move slightly forward. Her hand fluttered over her brow; she tucked an errant strand of blond hair into the loose bun at her nape. "Last night I attended a Mother's Against Drunk Drivers meeting."

"How did you feel?"

"Frustrated. MADD, DWI, DOA—they're like meaningless letters jumbled together in alphabet soup. When are the legislature and the courts going to do something? Look what happened in Jamie's case. It took weeks to connect the drunk driver with the accident. Although he'd previously been arrested twice for drunk driving, his license wasn't even suspended." Her eyes narrowed with anger. "With the slick lawyer he has, I don't think he'll spend a day behind bars. And what happens if he does go to prison? They rehabilitate him? Dry him out? Release him within six months?" Sara slapped his desk with the palm of her hand. "This is justice?"

Jared's brow puckered slightly; his wise blue eyes watched Sara intently through dark-framed glasses. "Your anger is healthy, Sara. First the hurt, then the anger. You're recovering. Are you still gathering signatures on petitions?"

"MADD is also collecting funds to pay a professional lobbyist. For whatever good that will do," she muttered, "congressmen drink. They show concern but don't pass stringent laws they have to live by."

"So? You're feeling angry and frustrated," Jared reiterated.

"And lonely . . . and guilty," she added, lowering her head.

"Have you talked to Mark recently?"

"I'm short on courage regarding Mark. He hates me. He probably thinks I belong in jail, sharing a cell with the drunk driver," she answered softly.

"Aren't you being hard on yourself and Mark? Taking a walk with your son can hardly be classified as neglect. A self-made, astute businessman who's known throughout the industry for his fairness wouldn't hold you responsible for the accident."

Sara abruptly rose from the chair and began pacing back and forth in the small office. "Business acumen doesn't preclude emotions. He may be whiz at making money," she explained further, "but that same logical mind sees our separation and my career as the cause of Jamie's death."

"Did he make those allegations?"

"No, but I'm sure it's what he thinks. Hell, maybe he's right. If I hadn't gone to that meeting after school, and if Jamie and I had taken our walk earlier, that maniac wouldn't have . . ." Sara was unable to finish.

"Sara, there are 'ifs' in everyone's life. Put them where they belong. If the driver's license

15

had been revoked earlier . . . if he hadn't been drunk . . . if he'd called a cab. The list is endless. Neither your career nor your separation from Mark caused the accident. Remember saying that? I'm quoting you." Jared moved from behind his desk, stopping in front of Sara. He placed his hands on her upper arms and quietly asked, "What's really behind this guilt?"

Sara's eyes sank to her toes. Jared had struck straight to the heart of her need to have an impartial person listen to her thoughts. And yet, now that he'd asked, she found her tongue unable to explain her immediate fear.

"Mark is coming over tonight," she replied, her muffled voice coming from below his chin.

"How do you feel about seeing him?"

Sara worried her bottom lip between her teeth. Should she tell Jared that after six months of being without Mark, the mere thought of seeing him made her heartbeat accelerate? Simply mentioning his name made the palms of her hands moist. Would he understand that the size of her bed seemed to have grown tenfold since Mark had gone?

She couldn't. Mark had walked out on her. These heated emotions were humiliating.

Where was her pride?

Deciding that the best defense was a good offense, she broke away from his gentle hold. "Don't psychologists ever have the *answers* to problems? All I get from you is questions!" Her chocolate-colored eyes snapped in anger. She could see from the expression on his face that her ploy hadn't worked.

"You have the answers. I can only help you think through your problems in search of them. Why don't you sit down? Let's work through this new crisis."

Taking her by the hand, he led Sara to the cushioned sofa. Jared sat down beside her. Elbows on her knees, Sara fingered the feathered bangs hanging over her forehead. When her fingers slowed their agitated plucking, Jared asked, "What about Mark?"

"I haven't talked to Mark since he lambasted me at the hospital. After he barged through the doors of the emergency room, he told me I needed to climb out of the Ivory Tower of Education and wake up to what was going on around me."

Salty dampness gathered behind her eyelids. She wouldn't cry. Tears were a weakness Sara seldom indulged in. She'd learned early in her career that male administrators scoffed at teary-eyed teachers. Leaving Jared's office with tears streaming down her face would be relayed quickly to the top echelon. Not by Jared, of course, but by another teacher or student. Sara cleared her throat and tasted the saltiness.

"Do you think Mark was as shocked as you at the time?"

"I don't know," she mumbled. "I suppose so."

"How do you feel about Mark now?"

Sara didn't want to answer his question. She didn't know how she felt about Mark Manchester.

To cope with Jamie's death she'd suspended any feelings about Mark into an emotional limbo.

"More questions?"

"Only if you want them, Sara. Teachers and psychologists are difficult patients. We try to feel with our heads instead of our hearts."

Sara lowered her eyes so Jared couldn't see them. Mark had said the same words when they had started dating. Prior to Mark, her life had been hidden under a pile of research books. The scope of her awareness had been narrow, centered around academic studies. She hadn't known how to play. In their four and a half years of marriage he'd taught the teacher how to live and laugh. With his sensuous tutelage she had become a woman with the same hopes, desires, fears, and frustrations of other women. She'd learned about love . . . and pain.

"Do you want to divorce Mark?" Jared asked in a straightforward, no-nonsense manner.

"No," she replied starkly. "I guess in my case, wanting a divorce is going to be like wanting to get married."

A puzzled frown creased Jared's forehead. "Didn't you want to get married?"

"I didn't have a choice. I was pregnant. We had to get married."

Surprised by her candor, Sara's head jerked upright. A pink tinge heightened her pale cheeks. Her eyes searched his face for condemnation.

Others had silently condemned her when they hid their fingers behind their backs and counted the months between marriage and birth. Her parents had told everyone that Jamie was premature to hide their disgrace.

"Silly for two grown people not to practice birth control, right?" she asked when she couldn't tell how he judged her.

"No. Not silly. Human."

A long sigh escaped her. "So," she said, elongating the single syllable, "now there is no child, no reason for Mark to remain married to me."

"Didn't you speak to Mark at the funeral or since then?"

"At Jamie's funeral I was numb. I couldn't tell you who was there or what was said. I couldn't face Mark."

"You know, there is the possibility that Mark also feels guilty."

Sara simply shook her head in denial.

Jared put his finger under her chin to stop the movement. "Men are taught to hide their emotions from early childhood. He may have the same doubts and fears that you have, but he's been trained to conceal them."

The idea of Mark feeling guilty was completely foreign to Sara. He didn't have any reason to feel guilty. Jamie had been in her sole care, not his.

"Mark is . . . well, hard to understand. In the years that we were married I'm not certain I ever truly knew what he was thinking. He said that he loved me, but I'm not sure about that now. One day he was there; the next he was gone."

"Acute communications problem?"

Sara shook her head. "We talked. But you're probably right. We never solved problems. I ig-

19

nored them. We didn't argue or fight because I was too scared. I loved him so much, I couldn't risk losing him."

"Do you still love him?"

The question hung between them for a long time. Did she love Mark? When they'd lived together, she'd taken her love for granted and worried about Mark loving her, worried about being the perfect wife and mother.

"Do I love him?" she whispered. "I can't answer that question the way I would have this time last year. I keep telling myself I shouldn't love him. It hurts too much to love." She shook her head again. "I honestly don't know."

Glancing at her watch, she levered herself out of the deep cushion. "I know you have a parent conference in five minutes." She laughed without mirth. "And I need to prepare myself for the firing squad. Thanks, Jared."

He took her hand between both of his. "Take care, Sara. Beth Ann sends her love. And remember, if you need me, I'm always here."

As she removed her hand and headed toward the door, Sara had a strange feeling of déjà vu. Had Mark said those same words at the grave site? He couldn't have. He hated her.

Sara scanned the parlor to make sure everything was immaculate. Mark had often praised her ability to keep an orderly house, take care of Jamie and himself, and work full-time. "Super Mom," Jamie had chimed, racing through the house with a feather duster, pretending he had a magical cape on his small shoulders. How she wished she could step back in a time warp and stay there.

Blinking back the tears hovering on her lashes, she eased herself into a red armchair. She loved this room. Each piece of furniture had been carefully chosen to complement the Victorian exterior. She and Mark had taken hours from their hectic schedules to shop together. As each piece was set in place, the strings of marriage had strengthened. How had their lives managed to unravel so quickly?

Her eyes focused on the empty fireplace where they had spent hours working side by side, stripping coats of white paint until the natural red of the brick reappeared. How many cold nights had Mark, Jamie, and herself sat watching the fire as they clicked together the pieces of Jamie's wooden puzzles? How many times had the three of them rollicked together, giggling and laughing, hugging and kissing, on the braided rug? Too many to count, Sara mused.

In her mind's eye she saw the flames dancing in the back of the grate. Jared's questions provoked her thoughts. Sara hadn't intended to tell Jared about why Mark married her, why he would be asking for a divorce. She recalled the night she had told him of her pregnancy.

She'd been scared. What if he laughed and said, "Tough. You're the college grad. You take care of it." Would he automatically assume responsibility? Or would she have to convince him that he was the father? Mortified at the prospect of having to prove he was the only man she'd ever made love with, she literally shook with fear the entire evening.

Parked in front of her apartment, Mark had coaxed the truth from her.

"We'll be married immediately," he had responded quietly.

No joy, no anger, no excitement was expressed, either verbally or physically. The next day he efficiently arranged for the blood tests. Three days later they stood before a judge and spoke their vows. The consequence of their physical act was legalized.

She'd often wondered if it was possible for a man to comprehend how being forced into a marriage caused a woman to miss hearing the words: Will you marry me? Those women had a choice. Sara had had none. She'd had to provide a legitimate name for their unborn child. Above all, the marriage had to be expedient.

Doubts led to the questions she had asked herself from the moment they'd left the judge's chambers. Did he love her? Would he have married her if she hadn't been pregnant? Did he want the child? Did she subconsciously want to get pregnant? She still wondered how Mark would have answered them.

Her fear of rejection, of knowing the truth, prevented her from voicing the questions.

As each month had passed, her body and fears increased proportionately. Her protruding stomach and lost waistline could no longer be politely ignored. Mark assured her she was beautiful, but she knew better. The mirror reflected how awkward and ungainly she appeared. Mirrors didn't lie.

During the last month of her pregnancy Mark had moved into the room they'd decorated as the nursery, claiming she'd be more comfortable. She hated sleeping alone. She had wanted to shout, "Don't leave me! I need you beside me!" Yet she hadn't. Wordlessly she'd gone to bed each night praying for a speedy delivery.

After Jamie was born, Mark took great pride in their son. His wallet bulged with baby pictures. The nursery was crammed with every imaginable toy. He loved Jamie. But did he love her? Could it be possible that she had been jealous of Jamie?

Sadly Sara shook her head. She knew Jamie had held their marriage together—for a while. In the end, Mark's love for Jamie wasn't strong enough. He'd left them.

She couldn't remember how or what had precipitated Mark's walking out. One minute she was anticipating rushing back from the PTA meeting in time to tuck Jamie into bed, and the next, Mark had gone. What had happened that night? Had she unconsciously goaded him into leaving? It wasn't the first time she'd had to attend a parent-teacher meeting at school.

The next day his clothes were gone. A curt note requesting weekend privileges with Jamie was all that remained of their marriage.

He wanted Jamie; he didn't want her.

She had poured her love on Jamie. That was a love she could trust. A child couldn't walk away from her and not return. Jamie responded with the warmth and openness Mark withheld. Without reserve Jamie loved her.

And a drunk driver destroyed that love.

Sara rubbed the back of her stiff neck. She had to loosen up or she'd be a jittery wreck when she faced Mark. Physical exertion, she thought decisively. What she needed was a fast run to unwind.

She glanced down at the pink jogging suit she'd slipped into when she came home from school. Mark wouldn't arrive for another two hours. She had time. By then, she'd be back, showered, and ready to face him. Sticking around the house dredging up old memories wouldn't help her face the inevitable. Mark was going to ask for a divorce. She had to pull herself together or her pride would be in the dust when she begged him to stay. She couldn't—wouldn't—allow herself to grovel.

Sara got the house key from her purse and stuck it in her pocket. She couldn't run away from Mark, nor could she run away from the past, but she could run away from her memories. For now that would suffice.

Mark used his key to open the door when Sara didn't respond to the door bell.

"Sara?" he called.

The house was quiet.

He closed the door and entered the living room. "Sara?"

Of all the things he'd prepared himself for, her not being there wasn't one of them. He had expected her to slam the door in his face and tell him to go away. Hadn't he heard those exact words all his life? The dirty kid from the slums of Dallas wasn't wanted.

Mark removed his coat, neatly hanging it on his hook. He rubbed his hands together as though washing them. He'd worked long and hard to scour the stink of poverty off his skin, but it was pointless. Underneath his strong, independent facade he knew he was the same unwanted, unclean kid he'd always been. A thin veneer of civilized manners covered the man he knew he was. Right now he could feel the hot blood coursing through his veins at the thought of being with Sara again. The primitive side of his nature wanted to find Sara, toss her on the bed, and get her pregnant again. He hadn't planned the first pregnancy, but at the time he couldn't deny being thankful that a big wedding that demanded the presence of his nonexistent family had been avoided.

His hands clenched in both pockets as a tremor of desire shot from his mind to his heart, then lower. Slowly he unclenched his hands and pulled them out. He stared at them, remembering Sara teasing him about them.

"Your hands are a dead giveaway. You shutter your eyes and cover your facial expressions like a professional gambler, but your hands don't lie."

He'd trained himself thereafter to keep them loose at his side. His stomach could be tied in knots, as it was the night he'd purposely picked a fight with Sara so he could leave without explanations, but his hands remained steady. He felt certain that nothing, neither his hands nor his mouth, had betrayed the precarious financial position his construction firm had been in when he'd left.

Months ago, when his business was on the brink of disaster due to the high interest rates and low building starts, he had fled rather than face Sara. Fear of failure kept him away. His blood ran cold at the mere thought of the loving warmth in her eyes changing to the same spiteful gaze he'd seen as a kid when the school cafeteria workers punched his free lunch pass. Free lunch? There was no such thing. He'd paid. For Mark the price of poverty was pride.

After he'd left Sara and Jamie he'd used every ounce of strength and cunning to keep the construction company he'd built from scratch running at a profit. He ate and slept at the shop. Managing each dollar carefully, cautiously, he'd survived while other companies folded. The money he had given Sara to support herself and Jamie was the only luxury he'd allowed himself.

But he had been unable to foresee the future. Just when he felt financially secure enough to reenter their lives, fate stepped in and dealt them a cruel blow. Jamie had been senselessly killed. Mark had gambled and lost. First Sara, then Jamie.

Dammit, he cursed silently, why Jamie? The world was full of scumbags . . . why not one of them? Or himself? Then at least Sara would have had Jamie.

If there was any justice, he thought, Sara would have another child to love. But before that could take place, he'd have to get through the hatred she felt toward him.

Mark didn't doubt that she despised him for the irrational things he'd said at the hospital. He'd let her down when she needed him most. He'd been out of his mind with despair. Now he'd cut his tongue from his mouth before uttering them, but then he'd allowed himself to wallow in self-pity. In his heart he knew he deserved any punishment life meted him, but not Sara. Not the woman who was everything good and sweet and beautiful to him.

After Jamie's death he vowed to make it up to her. His misplaced pride in his construction company had cost him dearly. Being president of Manchester Builders, the business he'd built with his own sweat, was too risky financially. Merging his company with a larger construction company would guarantee a bountiful supply of money. She could have anything her heart desired. He'd get it for her no matter what the cost.

Mark turned as he heard footsteps running up the front steps. He rammed his hands back into his pockets to hide the tremors that made them visibly shake. When he heard the key inserted into the lock, he stepped to the door and opened it.

Sara felt her mouth drop when she saw him. Panting from the strenuous run, gulping air through her open mouth, she knew with her hair wildly blown around her face that she looked frightful. An audible groan passed through her lips. What was he doing here over an hour early? This wasn't how she wanted to look when he arrived!

Letting her anger cover her embarrassment, she demanded, "What are you doing inside?"

"I rang the door bell. No one answered, so I used my key." His mind took a mental picture of how she looked with her hair mussed, her jogging suit stretching across her lush breasts as she drew air into her lungs, her chin tilted defiantly upward. God, she was beautiful.

Sara pulled her gaze away from his face. His dark hair, slightly rumpled as though he'd raked his hand through it, his clear blue eyes, his dimple that winked sensuously at her as he spoke, was debilitating. She quelled the urge to fling herself into his arms and beg his forgiveness. She couldn't do what she wanted most. Instead she straightened her shoulders and calmed her racing heart with one more deep breath.

"If you'll step aside and quit blocking the doorway, I'll join you in *my* home."

Determined not to let her rankle him, Mark smiled and said, "The Spanish have a polite greeting I'm partial to. My house is your house."

CHAPTER TWO

"Why couldn't you have arrived on time?" she blurted once she was inside. "You're always early!"

Mark shrugged; he hooked his thumbs into his belt loops. "Overanxious, maybe?"

"Overanxious?" she repeated incredulously. "You haven't communicated with me in months, then you send word via your secretary that you want to see me within twenty-four hours. That hardly depicts a man who's 'overanxious' to see his wife."

"Why don't I fix you a nice, tall drink while you run up and take a shower? Afterward we'll talk."

His placating, calm tone annoyed her even more. "Don't be condescending with me. You don't have to tell me I look awful. Sweat doesn't

29

affect how my brain functions. I'm able to conduct a conversation."

Sara knew she was being unreasonable and hostile, but the struggle to keep distance between them was wearing on her nerves. His being kind rather than angry, as she'd pictured him being, had knocked her completely off-balance. She glanced around the entryway looking for his briefcase, certain that the divorce papers would be stacked on top of his other business papers.

"I didn't arrive suitcase in hand," Mark said as he watched her eyes. "I didn't think it would be appropriate."

"Where's your briefcase?"

"I'm not here to conduct business."

"What *are* you here for?" she demanded, bewildered. She watched his hands curl into tight balls until ten white knuckles stretched the skin of his hands. Immediately they fell to his side and hung limply.

"I'm here to discuss our . . . marriage." Mark had to swallow before he could get the final word between his lips. "I think we should try again."

Sara stumbled backward as her head abruptly lifted. "What?"

"I said—"

"I heard you. I just don't believe what I heard. You can't walk in here and act as though nothing has happened!"

Mark forced himself to grin, hiding the fear tightening the muscles in his chest. "Why not? We're married. I do make the mortgage payments."

"Why not?" Her voice raised an octave. "Why not?"

"Don't overreact, Sara. One thing I've always admired about you is your serenity." Mark strolled into the living room as though he'd returned home from work and anticipated a warm welcome from his wife.

Grabbing his sleeve, Sara wheeled him around. In a low, controlled tone that covered the blood pounding in her ears, she informed him of her intentions. "Pardon me, but I'm not feeling *serene!* I'm going to go upstairs and take a shower. Then I'm going to come back down here and serenely explain why you can't move back into this house."

"The past is behind us, Sara." The arm she held snaked around her waist, drawing her close. "The only thing you need to remember is this."

Sara watched his lips as they slowly followed an invisible path to hers. Jerk away, she ordered herself. This is what had gotten her into his bed to begin with. Mesmerized by the warmth in his eyes, held loosely in his muscular arm, she didn't budge an inch.

His lips brushed hers, once, twice, savoring the salty flavor. "I've missed you," he mumbled against her parting lips.

Sara felt a familiar silken web of desire being woven around her. The hushed quality of his low voice beckoned her to forget anything other than the warmth of lips. He'd always been able to sway her to his way of thinking with soft words and

31

gentle caresses. Not this time, her mind feebly protested.

"No! I won't let this happen again!" Sara yanked herself away from him and ran up the steps. "It won't be that easy!"

Mark raked his index finger over his lower lip as though to seal her imprint on his mouth. Adopting his strong facade, he called after her, "Want me to scrub your back?"

Sara didn't dignify the question by responding until she was safely inside the master bedroom. "I'll scrub your face with the bristled edge of the brush if you do!"

The words had scarcely passed over her tongue when she realized that she was lying to herself. Taking showers together had been a sensual delight they'd often enjoyed.

"In the *past!*" she reminded herself.

As she removed her clothing she tried to assimilate what had taken place downstairs. Her heart fluttered when she realized that Mark had arrived without divorce papers. Did he mean it? Did he really want to return? Was that good fortune or misfortune? she wondered. Her life with Mark had been filled with ecstasy. She'd missed him with every fiber of her being. A swift pang of excruciating loneliness reminded her of what she'd be missing if she succeeded in forcing Mark to leave their house.

She couldn't let him come here and tie her up in knots, she thought as she went to the bathroom and turned on the shower. A kiss or two didn't make the hurt go away, and she couldn't ignore

32

problems anymore. This time they would *talk* about problems, and it wouldn't be *pillow talk!*

Sara stepped into the shower and scrubbed her face, but his kisses couldn't be washed away. She could still feel their warmth, their coaxing softness. Damn Mark. She couldn't let him do this to her! She couldn't pretend nothing happened! She wouldn't let him waltz back into her life, never knowing when the dance would end and he'd waltz back out again.

She grabbed the soap with her wet hand; it slipped from between her fingers and fell to the floor.

Downstairs, Mark stood in the kitchen with his head tilted toward the ceiling as he listened to the commotion overhead. Sara didn't stomp her feet, he thought as the sharp, bouncing noise occurred again. Maybe she'd fallen? His ears strained to hear any cry for help.

"You're searching for an excuse to go up there," he whispered, closing his eyes to fight his desire. Sara always had that effect on him. Small droplets of perspiration beaded along his upper lip.

With eyes closed he pictured her taking her shower. A low groan came from deep in his chest. His hand tightened on the edge of the counter. "Don't be a damned animal!" he said, chastising himself and forcing his eyelids open.

He pushed himself away from the counter and slowly began circling the dinette set. Their sexual attraction was mutual. God, he knew that. It was the single defense he had against her glibness.

She could take his own words and twist them into a new meaning. He couldn't depend on winning a verbal war, especially now. She'd come downstairs and demolish him with his own good intentions.

Deep in thought, he automatically removed his suit jacket and tie. His agile fingers flicked the buttons of his shirt open until it exposed the top half of his chest. He rolled up his sleeves, as he did at the office when he had a difficult problem to solve. He couldn't allow himself to be underhanded enough to fight this battle in the bed, could he?

His finger ran along his bottom lip. For a fraction of a second she had responded to him; he'd felt it. Perhaps he was being fair, but foolish, to depend on having a rational discussion with her. "I could win in the bedroom," he muttered. "I can be back where I belong."

The shower was still running. He could . . . No, he couldn't. Making love to Sara would be wonderful, but it would be a minor victory. She wouldn't allow him to act as though nothing had happened. Lord, he wished she would, but he knew better. He'd captured her once when she was unaware of what was taking place. Sara wouldn't fall into the same trap again.

He wouldn't fight dirty this time. Back-alley street tactics weren't something to be used on someone he loved. His hands fiddled with a button on his shirt. He was lying to himself. He'd do anything to get back in her good graces, to get back into her life.

34

Half an hour later, feeling clean and composed and dressed in apricot pants and a matching silk blouse, Sara entered the kitchen. Mark sat in a kitchen chair, balancing it on the two back legs.

"Four on the floor," she reminded him with her schoolmarmish voice.

The two front legs thudded to the linoleum. Mark winced, then glanced down at the twin black marks marring the polished surface. "Sorry. Old habits are hard to break."

Sara sat down in the chair across the table from him. "You won't be around long enough to break your bad habits again. I've thought this over and—"

"Raking our problems up, dissecting them, putting them under a microscope won't heal the hurts, Sara. Let's take what we have and go from there."

"What do we have?"

"You. Me. That simple."

"And that complicated," she rebutted, adding flippantly. "Sex doth not a marriage make."

"We agree. Sex is an easy commodity. We both want more." Mark knew from the way she carefully studied his face that he was saying the right thing. His confidence slipped when she suddenly frowned.

"You always considered me 'easy,' didn't you?" She moved to the edge of her chair, anticipating confirmation of her inner suspicions.

"Why do you ask? Because you were pregnant before we got married?" He chuckled to hide the nagging fear that one day she'd find out why he

35

had pushed for a hasty marriage. When that day occurred, he'd be out on his ear, fast. He leaned forward and captured her hand between his. "Honey, you were never easy."

"You can't discount the fact that lust played a major role in our getting married to begin with," she countered. A small, tingling current sent pleasurable sensations from her fingers to her heart. Deny it, Mark, her heart pleaded.

"Lust? Maybe." He grinned in a way that he knew tugged at her heartstrings. "If so, let's hear it for lust!"

Disappointed by the truth, she tugged her fingers to get them away from him. "Is it lust that brought you back?"

"That's a damned loaded question. You'll be angry if I tell you I'm not interested in having you in my bed, won't you? And if I tell you I want you, you'll twist that into meaning I need sex. Right?" Mark looked into her eyes.

Her lips drooped. "You're answering with questions," she reprimanded.

"I told you there wasn't any point in having a heavy discussion before making a decision. I'm merely following the example you set." Skirt the issue, he silently warned himself. He couldn't afford a face-to-face confrontation. He'd lose. "You're a good teacher." Mark patted her hand affectionately, then rose to his feet and headed toward the kitchen door.

"Where are you going?"

"To the car." He winked with seemingly audacious self-confidence.

"What for?"

"To get something for you . . . and my suit-cases."

He was gone before she could react. A split second later, she was following his footsteps. "Now you listen to me, Mark Manchester. You can't—" Her monologue was ended as the door closed when she rounded the corner.

Sara ran to the door and flung it open. "We haven't finished talking!"

"I have. Want to help me carry my bags in?"

She slammed the door and leaned against it, her arms folded across her chest. He couldn't just move in and move out every time the whim caught his fancy. By God, he may have been satis-fied with their discussions, but she wasn't. She wanted to get underneath that facade and bring the truth out into the open!

"Sara, I have a key. Let's not make a scene for the neighbors to enjoy."

"To hell with the neighbors!"

"There's a junior-high kid walking down the sidewalk. Do you want him to spread it around school tomorrow that—"

She stepped away from the door and opened it.

Mark entered with a mink stole draped over one shoulder and a suitcase in each hand. Setting the cases down, he whirled the cape toward her. "Happy Easter from your friendly hubby bunny," he said teasingly, delighted to have caught her off-guard again.

Sara wasn't about to let him buy his way back into their house. He'd always brought her little

37

gifts when he'd been guilty of some minor infraction. After nearly five years of marriage didn't he realize that it was the humble apology that made her draw him close, not the gift? The simple words *I'm sorry* hadn't been exchanged by either of them.

She tossed the fur back into his arms. "You wear it. It looks better on you."

Mark looked at the luxurious fur. "You think so? Well, I'll hang it in the closet and you can wear it when I don't."

"Very funny, Mr. Manchester, but you aren't going to sidetrack me with jokes or gifts. You aren't moving back in."

"Honey, I don't want to argue with you, but I am in." He swaggered into the living room, sat down in the leather wing chair, and propped his feet up on the matching ottoman. "To stay."

The image of a predatory beast entrenched in his lair flashed through Sara's mind. "Shall I have the police get you out of here?" Sara asked while picking up the phone on the end table. She added with bitter sweetness, "Surely four of St. Charles's finest will be able to evict you."

"You'll make a laughingstock out of yourself if you place that call," he said, warning her softly. "We aren't divorced. We aren't even legally separated."

"Everybody in town knows you no longer live here."

"Would you like everyone to know that I came bearing gifts, got down on bended knee, and you pushed me back through the front door?"

Sara shivered. She remembered the comments she'd heard during the past few months. Junior-high kids relished seeing an authoritarian figure hurt, and even some of her colleagues had talked behind her back. Whether crude, crass, or in between, Sara abhorred the thought of the failure of her marriage being the main topic of conversation at school.

"No."

"In that case, I'm staying. You *are* my wife."

"But for how long?" she muttered to herself as she walked back into the kitchen. Pausing at the swinging door, she rested her forehead on her knuckles as she tried to gather her wits. How long?

The hidden fear that she couldn't directly voice to Mark lay at the bottom of their troubles.

She entered the kitchen and crossed to the window over the kitchen sink. The sun streaming through the window was momentarily blotted by a gray, threatening cloud. She watched the gray mass move eastward. The sun broke through briefly before being hidden by another rapidly moving cloud. A storm was in the offing.

A distasteful odor coming from the sink drew her gaze downward. She flipped the garbage disposal switch. For a second she heard metal scrape and grind, then there was an ominous buzz. With a laugh bordering on hysteria, she pounded the Formica counter with an open palm.

Mark Manchester could fix it. He couldn't fix her heart, which was on the verge of being broken again, but he could fix the damned garbage disposal.

"Problem?" Mark asked from the doorway.

Sara pushed the switch down and the grating noise stopped. She moved away from the sink. "Another mechanical marvel of the building industry isn't working properly," she answered sarcastically.

Mark strode to the sink, pulled the rubber protector aside, and inserted his fingers. He plucked a misshapen fork from the disposal. "The mechanical world operates smoothly when obstructive obstacles are removed."

Grabbing the fork, completely aware of the ongoing double-talk, she tossed the fork into the trash.

"And when obstructive obstacles are no longer *useful,* they're thrown away," she replied caustically. His determination to return to hearth and home had to have a reason behind it. If he loved her, he wouldn't have walked out in the first place. He wanted something; she just didn't know what.

Mark watched the fork as it bounced in the bottom of the empty container. Did she consider him no longer useful? Trash? He turned and searched her eyes for a hidden meaning; he saw none.

"Only if they're beyond repair," he rejoined quietly. "Our marriage isn't beyond repair, sweetheart. By hook or crook I'm going to live here." His voice became clipped with determination. "I don't care what I have to do to reach that goal. Blackmail, brute force, whatever, I'll do it."

"Humph!" Sara scoffed, unimpressed with his ruthless claim. He might threaten physical or emotional violence, but she knew him too well to acknowledge the gauntlet he had thrown down.

"I mean it, Sara. I'll do whatever it takes. The end justifies the means."

Sara blinked, surprised. This was a facet of his character she had never seen. Had his business success been based on this same ruthlessness? How could she sidestep such determination? She'd have to make stipulations that would make their living together bearable.

"If I agree to you living here"—she paused to eliminate the wavering quality of her voice— "you'll have to sleep on the living room sofa."

"You expect my six-foot-four body to get any rest on a five-foot sofa? Don't be ridiculous. You didn't move the bed I bought from the master suite, did you?"

"You aren't sharing my bed; I don't give a hoot who paid for it. You're the one upsetting the apple cart. You can buy another bed and sleep in Jamie's room," she blurted without thinking of the consequences.

The pain that flashed across his face hurt her as badly as it had wounded him. Jamie. Would he be able to sleep in Jamie's room? Or would his dreams turn to nightmares? Her heart reached out to him, but she couldn't retract her stipulation.

41

"Agreed," Mark replied. "I'll have a bed delivered within the hour."

Unwilling to give Sara an opportunity to change her mind, Mark pivoted and left the room. He had to leave before Sara realized how weak he was. Living in the same house and being denied the privilege of touching her wouldn't be any worse than the hell of entering Jamie's room knowing that his boy wouldn't rush to him and fling his arms around his neck. Hell was hell. There wasn't any varying degrees. He wasn't bargaining from strength, he was bargaining from behind a huge bluff.

Sara wiped the tears from her eyes. "I could move!" she shouted, searching for an escape clause.

"You won't," she heard from the hallway.

"Of all the overbearing, high-handed . . ." she sputtered, pushing the swinging door aside.

Mark stood with the phone between his shoulder and ear, his finger on the push buttons. "Ungentlemanly, crude, rough," he added to her growing list. "Whatever it takes. In the business world I have two choices about failure. I can walk away from it and accept the loss or through sheer determination pull the fat from the fire and make a loser a winner. Walking away from you didn't work. Sheer determination will," he stated emphatically.

"I can't accept that."

"You will, honey. You will." His finger pushed the numbers of a local furniture store he had done business with in the past.

As she listened to him place the order for a bed, she realized that Mark relentlessly broke through any defenses she tried to erect. For her to lose in verbal sparring was an unknown element in their relationship. By twisting her words, forcing her to accept him into the house, Mark had drawn the lines and dared her to cross them. She was boxed in—at least for the time being.

CHAPTER THREE

Mark was placing his order for the bed over the telephone when he heard Sara climb the hallway steps. Delivery would be made within the hour, the salesman promised. A small smile of satisfaction hovered on his lips. Shortly he'd be residing permanently with Sara.

He lifted his suitcases and headed upstairs. The remote chance of Sara busily preparing the bedroom didn't occur to him. He mentally substituted spare room for Jamie's room. Sweeping the dust and making his own bed was a small sacrifice, he mused, walking down the hall.

Sara heard Mark's footsteps but couldn't turn away from the doorway to her son's room. Jamie's toys were there, just as he'd left them. She'd promised herself time and again to pack them up and donate them to a worthy organization, but each time she'd entered his room, she'd lost heart.

Giving the toys away and clearing his room made Jamie's death permanent. He wouldn't be back to line his G.I. Joe figurines for imaginary battles. He wouldn't play the stack of story records still on the phonograph. He wouldn't be there to build more Legg-O spaceships.

"Sara?" Mark's heart ached as he watched her lean against the doorjamb, then slowly slide down its length until she resembled a small, tight ball of pain. His eyes clouded as he glanced into the room. He realized that she hadn't touched anything. He wasn't certain that he could, either. But he had to, he told himself. Sara had borne the brunt of their loss. He had to shift the load to his shoulders. "You go downstairs. I'll take care of this."

"I meant to pack up his things," she whispered.

"I'll do it."

Sara raised her head. "It's so hard without him. I miss him."

"I know, sweetheart." And he did, but Sara needed his strength, not his pity. "Why don't you—"

She shook her head as she moved on all fours to the small metal cars near the door. "I'll help."

Mark couldn't argue. He wasn't certain that he could accomplish the task by himself. "We'll do it together."

Neither of them spoke as Mark went down the hallway to the hatch leading to the attic and pulled the dangling cord downward. The hatch opened and the folding stairs fell forward. Mark climbed them, wishing he could stay in the solitude of the attic and cry his eyes out. He gathered up the cardboard cartons they'd stored there and took them to Jamie's room.

They both packed up their son's belongings, each immersed in thoughts of the child they'd lost, each too choked up to speak, to share their private memories.

Sara closed the lid on a box of Dr. Seuss books. She struggled to block the sound of Jamie merrily giggling at the rhyming stories. She glanced at Mark. His hands shook as he wedged a football he'd given Jamie the previous Christmas into another box. A thin white line circled his compressed lips. In the entire time she'd lived with Mark he'd never verbally expressed anything that bothered him. He suffered in silence with only his hands betraying his feelings.

"You need to talk about it instead of bottling up your pain," she whispered.

"I can't."

"I had to talk to Jared Bishop. Didn't you share your grief with anyone?"

"No." Mark's hands froze in midair as he reached for a snapshot of the three of them at the St. Louis zoo. Talk? How could he tell a stranger what it felt like to emotionally bleed to death and still survive? They'd think he was crazy.

Sighing, she noticed a muscle along his jaw nervously twitching. "Can you talk to me?"

Talking to Sara meant bearing his soul. She was the last person he wanted to ridicule him.

She'd despise him for his weakness. A man had to be strong. Someone for Sara to cling to, not the person doing the clinging.

He kept his back toward her. "No, I can't talk about it. Let's just finish packing, okay?"

She knew Mark needed to talk, but she didn't know how to console him. Slowly she rose to her feet. She did know how, she reminded herself as she moved toward him. With infinite compassion she wrapped her arms around his waist and laid her face against his back. "It hurts like hell."

Closing his eyes, Mark felt tears stinging them. His large hands enveloped her slender hands. Once, long ago, he remembered being comforted by gentle hands. He hadn't been much older than Jamie when he'd tripped on his shoestring at the school playground and fallen. The kindergarten teacher on playground duty had rushed to him. As though it happened yesterday, he remembered watching her raise his ragged pant leg and tenderly cover his knee with a linen handkerchief edged with lace. He knew she'd ruined it. Ruined it for a kid she didn't even know. He'd cried then. Not because of his skinned knee but because of her gentleness. She'd insisted that he keep the handkerchief. That afternoon he'd scrubbed it in the school bathroom sink until only a trace of stain remained. He'd carried it in his pocket until it was frayed and threadbare. But he hadn't forgotten the shred of kindness in his bleak childhood.

Mark cleared his throat, tasting the saltiness of his own tears.

"Yeah, it hurts like hell," he echoed. "But we'll have other children."

Sara abruptly pulled away from Mark. He made Jamie sound as though he'd been a puppy that had been run over. She didn't want another puppy. She didn't want another child who could be cruelly taken from her.

"I don't think so," she whispered, turning, picking up the box she'd finished packing, and taking it to the doorway.

Her abrupt withdrawal left Mark feeling fragile, close to shattering. To hide his weakness he smiled, thumping the wall between the master bedroom and the room they were in. "Not with this between us, huh?"

"That wall isn't the major barrier separating us," she said sadly. "I'm not going to have another unwanted child."

"Unwanted?" Mark retorted. "Can you honestly say I didn't want Jamie? That I was a bad father?"

"I didn't mean to imply—"

"Well, it sure as hell sounded as though you thought I were unfit!" Mark roared.

Shocked by his raised voice, Sara matched his volume. "You were a great father—when you were here!"

A red tide of anger flushed over Mark's dark complexion. "Now just a goddamn minute. I religiously sent money. I didn't miss a weekend of being with Jamie."

"Money doesn't replace love! And a weekend

doesn't make up for the rest of the week when he missed you!"

"I couldn't give you more money, or Jamie more time," Mark stated solemnly, his voice barely above a whisper.

"Why? Didn't you love him enough? Was stockpiling money more important than being with your son?"

"I just couldn't. Forget it. It's water under the bridge."

Sara dropped the box of books she'd been holding tightly against her chest and stormed back into the room. She saw the impenetrable mask behind which he hid slip into place and she wanted to pound her fists against him in frustration. Feet spread as though balanced for a defeating blow, she blasted, "It's not likely that I'm going to forget it. There won't be any other children for you to turn your back on. Not with me! Maybe you'd better change your decision to return. Go find yourself another dumb, naive woman to get pregnant. While you were gone, this one grew up!"

Mark grabbed her wrists to keep her from leaving. The gamble he'd taken by returning was doomed to failure unless he played his wild card. "Can you honestly say you don't love me?"

"Yes!" she hissed.

"Then say it." He transferred her wrist into one hand, freeing the other to raise her chin. "Say it, sweetheart. Say it now, mean it, and I'll leave. You'll never see or hear from me again."

The thought of him keeping his promise

49

drained her anger, leaving her face pale. It wasn't an idle threat. "I don't . . ."

"Say it all." His eyes blazed with pain. "Mark, I don't love you."

She struggled to repeat the five simple words. "Mark . . . I—"

His fingers pressed against her lips. "Shh. Don't say them, Sara, please. God, I'll die if you say them."

Sara could only look at him silently, stunned by his words. She knew how much they had cost him. He wasn't a man who begged.

It would be so easy to kiss his fingertips and confess how much she loved him, because she realized that she did love him. So easy, she mused as she bowed her head. But she'd taken the easy road years ago when she shifted the responsibility of her pregnancy on him. The easy road was filled with emotional pot holes and led to a dead end. There were no easy roads in life.

"I want you to stay," she finally whispered.

Mark pulled her into his arms, crushing her against his chest, expelling the breath he'd been holding. He wanted to absorb her goodness into himself, making him cleaner, better than what he'd been born to be.

The door bell broke them apart.

"Your bed has arrived," Sara said, her voice shaking.

"Do I need it? Can't . . ."

Sara expected his question but couldn't risk closer involvement with him. She'd found the answer to Jared Bishop's question. She did love

50

him, yet she couldn't allow him to be an intimate part of her life when the fear of his departure hung between them. She still didn't know why he'd walked out.

"I'll let them in," she said between tight lips, choking.

She went downstairs and opened the door, struggling to act as though having a double bed delivered for her husband were an everyday occasion. Mark saved her from embarrassment by calling to the men from the top of the hallway and telling them that he'd show them where to set it up.

Mark was staying. Her heartbeat accelerated as the joy spread throughout her body. He wanted to stay. He'd practically begged to stay. Mark beg? That was certainly something new and different for him. His stoic, suffer-in-silence attitude would have been more like him. Maybe this time they'd be able to communicate with each other.

Jamie's death had been a tragedy, but maybe they could build something from their loss.

Hope, like the spring sunshine, warmed her.

She glanced upward as she heard male chuckles spilling from the spare bedroom. Inwardly she winced. Were they joking about she and Mark having separate bedrooms? No, she knew they weren't. Mark verbalizing about needing her was a far cry from him destroying his masculine image by admitting that he and his wife didn't share the bed in the other room.

Feeling foolish standing in the entryway listening to the men's bantering exchange upstairs,

Sara went into the kitchen and started preparing dinner. One of the hardest parts about coming home each night after work had been eating by herself. But now that Mark was back, she was actually looking forward to dinner.

Mark thanked the men for the prompt delivery and strode toward the aroma coming from the kitchen.

"I'd planned on taking you to Five Flags for dinner," he said as he watched her move from the stove to the sink.

"Thanks, but dinner is almost ready."

"I'll set the table," he offered.

He'd never told Sara how much he had appreciated her having dinner ready for him each night when he came home from work. She'd be shocked if she knew how irregularly he'd eaten as a kid.

Welfare checks came once a month. On that day, usually a Saturday, he and his mother would go to the grocery store—if she was sober. More often than not, he went to the store by himself. They'd spend an allotted amount on food. Food stamps had helped.

Mark remembered gorging himself on that day, with good reason. Usually, the last of the month's groceries and the end of the month never coincided. The free lunch at school often was all he'd had to eat for a week or more. In the summertime, when there were no free lunches, he'd starve or find odd jobs rather than do what other kids in his predicament had to do: steal.

No, he mused, Sara might joke when they were

late sitting down to a meal by saying that she was starving, but she didn't have any idea what real stomach-to-backbone hunger was all about.

Sara poured the green beans from the pot into the bowl. Using two hot pads, she picked up the vegetable and crossed to the table. Both hands jerked, spilling the beans as she glanced at the table. She gasped but couldn't set the bowl on the table or make it back to the counter.

He'd set the table for three.

Mark, seeing his error, quickly removed one place setting, then took the bowl from her hands.

"Habit," he explained. Remorse drew his lips downward. "I was thinking of something else."

Sara crumpled into her chair. She'd done it too. How many nights had she wept as she put the knife and fork back into the drawer? She watched Mark's face stiffen, keeping his composure at all costs.

"I'm sorry," he mumbled.

"Me too."

To keep her hands busy, Sara began dishing the food. Her vow not to let Mark get close enough to hurt her waned. When two people shared the same agonizing loss, it was difficult to think in terms of punishment or revenge.

"So how's business?" she asked, trying to restore a fragment of normalcy.

Mark sat down after returning the place setting to the silverware drawer. His fingers tingled as though severely burned by his error. "On the upswing. How's school?"

"Crazier than usual. You know how the kids are

53

when the weather gets warm." She smiled weakly as she added an old line she'd said each spring. "On May Day they should call off school for lack of interest."

Mark grinned. "Didn't you have Hal Moran's boy in your class a few years ago?"

"Uh-huh. Nice boy. A bit straitlaced, but I understood once I met his parents. "Why?" Sara sliced her pork chop. When she took her first bite, she realized that food hadn't tasted that good in a long time.

"Hal and I are in the midst of negotiations."

"Oh, Mr. Moran owns Moran Construction, doesn't he? I'd think you'd be in competition rather than in negotiations. I read in the paper that he bought a large tract of land in St. Peters. What are you going to do? Build houses in the same subdivision?"

The two of them seldom discussed business. She had no mechanical aptitude, and Mark wasn't interested in designing curricula. Sarah viewed their conversation as a good sign. Perhaps they could communicate on more than a physical level if they both tried.

"Something like that," Mark replied evasively. "Pass the salt, please."

The tips of his fingers brushed hers as she handed him the shaker. Their eyes met. Hers dropped to her plate, to hide her reaction to the tiny electric sparks that had passed between them.

"Mr. Moran makes his uptight kid look like the

town hood in comparison," she quipped, leading the conversation back on course.

"I don't think St. Charles has *hoods* anymore, does it?" Mark said teasingly.

Sara chuckled. "You know what I mean. Hal Moran has black-and-white perception. There are no grays in life as far as he's concerned. Better make certain your crews are clean-cut, wear uniforms, and wash their mouths daily with soap."

"Excluding the mouth washings, my crew fits the bill. I think that's why he's interested in merging."

"You're considering merging with Moran Construction? I thought you liked being your own boss." Sara's mind was three steps ahead of her mouth. Hal Moran was so far right, he was out of touch with modern society. If Mr. Moran approached Mark about consolidating their companies, she knew Moran had done a careful check into Mark's life. Mr. Moran wouldn't approve of an estranged marriage. To him, separation would be a gray area of life that could lead to a black smudge.

Sara didn't want to connect the obvious links together, but she couldn't escape the glaring facts. Was Mark's return to her predicated by the possible merger with Moran Construction?

"This year I learned some hard lessons about the construction business. It takes more than quality work and honesty to survive. It takes cash flow."

"So you're considering merging with Moran for the money?"

She lowered her fork to her plate as her appetite fled.

Money. That's why he'd returned. Her eyes narrowed at the realization. No wonder he wasn't distressed about not sharing the bedroom. As far as Mr. Moran was concerned, if they shared the same house, that was enough. Sharing the same bed wasn't important.

A year ago she would have changed the subject rather than confront Mark with her suspicions. Hadn't she made a claim earlier that while he'd been gone, she'd grown up? Dodging the issue smacked of immaturity.

Before Mark had an opportunity to answer, she bluntly asked, "Does merging with Moran have anything to do with your return?"

Mark continued to chew his food, swallowing before answering. *Everything,* he wanted to reply. Had he approached Moran a year ago, he wouldn't have been on the verge of filing for bankruptcy. He wouldn't have had to walk away from the two people who meant more to him than life itself. He would have been playing with Jamie, safe in their home on the night of the accident. His financial worries would have been nonexistent. But he hadn't approached Moran because of his pride, his determination to be his own man.

To hell with all that, he thought, financial stability was top priority. He'd rather have Sara's eyes snapping angrily at him than filled with pity or despising him for his failure.

"Yes," he honestly replied.

"Would you have returned if you weren't close to finalizing the deal?" Her words held a double-edged razor sharpness, inflicting painful wounds on her self-esteem. But she had to know. She couldn't avoid unpleasant truths.

Mark couldn't lie to her. He could see that acknowledging the connection displeased her, but he had to be truthful regarding the consolidation. In her present mood she'd probe until she discovered the whole truth. Then her eyes would change. He'd face her wrath before he explained his fear of poverty.

"Probably not. I won't minimize the importance of this merger."

"Hal Moran doesn't approve of a man and wife in separate residence, does he?"

"No, but neither does Mark Manchester. The minute I stepped out the front door with the suitcases in my hand, I wanted to come back."

"Why didn't you?" Sara said, parrying.

Mark shrugged, feeling the probe dangerously close to uncovering the slum kid. "I did what I thought was best."

Picking up his plate, he moved to the sink and rinsed it off. He flicked the switch on the garbage disposal. "Seems to be working fine now," he commented inanely.

On the tip of her tongue was one question Sara couldn't ask: Did he love her?

She didn't have to voice it. Hadn't he already made his reply glaringly clear? He'd returned, not because he loved her, not because he wanted to reunite, but because of a business merger. The deal wouldn't go through unless Mark gave the impression of marital stability.

Sara's chair scraped the kitchen floor as she pushed back from the table.

"I have papers to grade," she said, excusing herself.

Taking the steps two at a time, she raced for the sanctity of the bedroom. She didn't bother to lock the door before she flung herself on the bed. Why would she? Mark wasn't interested in her. Sure, she thought, a little sex on the side would be an added bonus for the big merger, but Mark wouldn't press the issue. He didn't have to hand Mr. Moran a certified statement of their bedroom activities!

She mentally cursed herself for being suckered into feeling compassion for Mark. For a while she'd actually believed that Mark had grieved over their loss. No wonder he couldn't talk about it. He was probably hard-pressed to appear grieved. Grieved? The coldhearted, materialistic bastard had probably planned each touching gesture.

She should have told him to leave when he'd given her the chance.

Her knuckles pressed against the lips he'd so tenderly kissed as he begged her not to ban him from the house. She should have known right then that he was playing a part. Mark Manchester didn't beg. What a sentimental fool she was!

At least she'd had sense enough to find the reason behind his sudden return. She couldn't

58

forcefully evict Mark, but she didn't have to win the Gullible of the Year Award by believing his act. Well, he wasn't the only one who could play a role to the hilt.

He'd never have the satisfaction of knowing what a knucklehead she'd been.

But how would she keep him from knowing that she loved him? He hadn't been back an hour before she'd rushed into the kitchen to fix him dinner. She'd been the one who had lovingly wrapped her arms around him, inviting his caresses. He could tell by looking at her that she still wanted him, craved his touch.

Toughen up, she coached herself. Adopt a page out of his book and mask those feelings behind a cool, brittle facade.

The sound of heavy footsteps coming up the stairs alerted Sara. She rose from the bed and hastily moved to the desk by the window. She might as well begin practicing what she'd preached. Hastily she opened her grade book, picked up a red pencil, and leafed through the stack of student papers.

"Sara," she heard from outside the door. "I've brought you a cup of coffee."

Stay out, she wanted to scream but didn't. Even that bit of emotion would reveal too much. "No, thanks."

"Can I get you anything?"

Sara had several thoughts ranging from pure sarcasm to the truth, but she coolly responded, "No, thanks."

Her head turned when she heard the door open.

"I don't suppose you'd reconsider about where I sleep, would you?" Mark asked, smiling wistfully.

Turning back around, she flipped through the papers. "No."

Mark crossed the room and set the mug of coffee on the desk. "I missed you."

Without so much as glancing up she serenely replied, "And I missed you."

"I'd rather sleep in here."

The enticing huskiness of his voice tempted Sara to look at him. Could he fake passion as easily as he faked grief? She avoided temptation by circling a glaring grammar error on the paper.

Mark stood behind her, nervously rubbing his hands together. "I didn't really expect you to sleep with me."

"Then you aren't disappointed."

Mark gently placed his hands on her shoulders; Sara shrugged them off.

"I'll be patient."

"Patience is a virtue," she quipped. Her hand covered her heart, as if to muffle the sound of its pounding.

"And virtue is rewarded?" Mark doubtfully asked. His tormented eyes focused on the crown of her head. He wanted to bury his hands in the soft silky curls, but he didn't dare. He deserved punishment. He hadn't been there when she needed him. He had to prove himself worthy of her love.

Patience, he reminded himself. To a hungry man patience and procrastination were the same. A hungry man took what he wanted. Mark blinked. A hungry *animal* took what it wanted. He wasn't an animal. Dammit, he wasn't, not with Sara.

Sara didn't reply.

Mark backed toward the door, silently praying for the strength to allow him to leave the room before his needs overwhelmed him. "Sweet dreams, love," he whispered inaudibly.

The latch clicking shut sapped the rigidness from her shoulders. Folding her arms on top of the papers, Sara sagged, resting her forehead against them. She shivered. Without his warmth in the room she was bone-cold.

Toughen up, she mouthed, rubbing the goose bumps on her arms. Toughen up.

CHAPTER FOUR

"Busy?"

Sara glanced to the doorway of her classroom and saw Jared Bishop. "Never too busy for you. What brings you up to the second floor?"

"You. I wanted to remind you about the anniversary party Beth Ann is having for us and to pry into your private affairs by asking how everything went last night."

"Mark's moved back into the house."

Jared sat on the corner of the desk. "The dark circles under your eyes I can chalk up to a long, blissful night. But where's the sunny smile?"

"I said he moved back in, I didn't say we were living together."

"That's about as clear as the muddy Mississippi. You're living together but you're not living together?"

Sara watched him poke his glasses higher on his nose with his forefinger. "Mark is negotiating a merger of his construction company with Hal Moran's company. To keep up appearances Mark moved into the spare bedroom."

"Hal Moran? I counseled his son."

"River water getting clearer?"

"Crystal clear. But surely Mark didn't arrive bag and baggage with the merger papers in his hand. You wouldn't have let him in the door."

"He has his own key. You've met Mark; I'm not capable of physically ousting him."

"You could change the locks."

"He'd have a locksmith there in five minutes flat. Mark's determined to push this merger through, regardless of the cost." Sara closed her lesson-plan book to emphasize the finality of Mark's decision.

"How do you feel about his being there?"

Sara pushed back her chair and stood. "Old buddy, I'm too tired for Twenty Questions today. Do you mind?"

"Of course not." He put his arm around Sara's shoulders. "I'm concerned about you."

"I'll manage." Sara sighed softly as she put her arm around his waist. Forcing herself to smile, she said, "I'll get a good night's sleep and be at your house tomorrow night with bells on my toes. Okay?"

"You don't have to put up a brave front for me." Jared gave her shoulders a light squeeze and said, teasing, "We love you even when you're a grump."

Sara was about to make a quip about being glad that he included his wife's love in that statement when out of the corner of her eye she saw Mark in the doorway. The murderous look in his blue eyes made her arm drop from Jared's waist as she abruptly moved away from him.

Mark could feel the thorns of the roses in his right hand digging into his flesh. He welcomed the pain. It distracted him from the impulse to smash the guy into the blackboard.

Jared followed the path of Sara's eyes. Smiling, he walked to the door, extending his hand. "I'm Jared Bishop. We met years ago at a faculty dinner."

Shifting the flowers to his left hand, Mark politely but silently shook hands. He quelled the urge to grind Jared's hand to a pulp.

"I've heard a lot about you since then," Jared said, in an effort to warm the iciness in Mark's eyes.

"Sara hasn't mentioned you." His civilized veneer stretched thinly over his reply.

Mark felt his gut wrench. The last thing he had expected from Sara was involvement with an older man. Desperately he tried to excuse what he'd overheard, but how could either of them explain Jared saying he loved her? They couldn't. Hell, they weren't even trying.

"What are you doing here, Mark? You've never picked me up from school."

"You left the house this morning, but your car was in the garage. I thought I'd surprise you." *And I was the one surprised*, he added silently. He

64

felt like the kid who'd spent his last dime on an apple for the teacher, and when he'd stayed after school to give it to her, he found her eating a bigger, juicier apple.

Jared shifted uncomfortably from one foot to another. The underlying current beneath the polite exchange between Sara and her husband made the hair on the back of his neck rise. "I was just leaving. Nice meeting you, Mark. Sara, I'll see you tomorrow night. Bring Mark if you like."

Sara nodded. Mark didn't move a muscle, for fear of decking him.

"I prefer to walk," Sara stated calmly when she knew that Jared was out of hearing range.

"The dismissal bell rang two hours ago." Mark tossed the long-stemmed roses on her desk. "Why aren't you home?"

"I worked late." She pushed the roses aside and placed her lesson-plan book in the center desk drawer. "I seem to recall you working late often."

Mark glanced at the doorway. "Working late? Standard euphemism for—"

"Shut up, Mark. You don't know what you're talking about."

"I won't close my mouth *or* turn a blind eye to you openly conducting an affair."

Between clenched teeth she corrected his assumption. "I am not having, nor have I ever had, an affair with Jared Bishop."

"Don't lie. I wondered why you never contacted me while we were separated. I was the one who always called to make arrangements to see Jamie."

"You were the one who walked out, remember?"

"Ah, but you had someone waiting on the sidelines, didn't you?" Mark rested his knuckles on the desk and leaned forward. "I won't tolerate you seeing another man."

"Why? Wouldn't Hal Moran approve? Would your precious merger fall through?"

"Our future depends on that merger."

"Don't you mean *your* future? The minute Moran puts his signature on the dotted line, you'll be gone."

"That's not true."

"Prove it. When we get to the house, call Moran and tell him the deal is off."

"I can't. I've verbally agreed to—"

"Heaven forbid you should break your word."

"I'll break Bishop's skinny neck if you go to his house tomorrow night."

The rage storming in his eyes left Sara with little doubt that he meant what he said. "It's his anniversary. He and his wife, Beth Ann, have been married for twenty-five years."

Mark turned abruptly and walked to the window. Married twenty-five years, he silently repeated, doubting that his marriage would last another twenty-five minutes if he continued to bungle everything. Hands on his hips, he sucked air into his lungs as though he'd run long and hard but lost the race.

"I was jealous," he admitted solemnly. "I

66

heard you say you'd be with him tomorrow night with bells on your toes and saw you smiling at him the way you used to smile at me. I wanted to smash his face."

Sara rubbed her forehead, silently understanding how he could have misinterpreted what he'd seen.

"I heard him say he loved you. That was the clincher." Mark swallowed, clearing the knot of rage in his throat. He was no longer angry with Sara, only himself. Although older, Jared Bishop was the type of man Sara should have married. Handsome, intelligent, part of the academic world she lived in. As much as he loved her, he couldn't free her to find a man like that. "I apologize."

"I accept your apology." Sara picked her keys from her purse and moved toward the door. "I have a meeting at six-thirty. I'd appreciate a ride home."

Mark schooled his face into an impassive mask and turned toward Sara. "You forgot your roses," he noted, picking them up from the desk and handing them to her.

She started to refuse them but changed her mind. One major battle a day was more than her quota. She accepted the gift with half a smile. When would he learn that he couldn't buy love with money? He'd never learn, she mused sadly. Money was his top priority. His lavish generosity didn't stem from love but from guilt.

"PTA on Thursday night? Have they switched

from Monday night meetings?" Mark asked as he opened the car door.

"Mother's Against Drunk Drivers meeting."

The title of the group excluded him. "A worthwhile group. Can I contribute?"

"Money?" Sara asked as she lifted the hem of her full skirt into her lap. "Why don't you donate your time?"

Mark closed the door and circled the car. After he started the engine and pulled from the parking lot, he asked, "Wouldn't a monetary contribution be of greater value than my time?"

"Not necessarily. We're gathering signatures on a petition to present to the state legislature. The representatives know that when election time rolls around and they haven't tightened the loopholes in the law, they're in danger of being voted out of office."

"Give me a stack of petitions. I'll do what I can," Mark promised.

Sara lowered her lashes and covertly glanced at him. The lines marring his brow hadn't been there last year. His lips, which had so easily laughed, drooped down at the corners. There was an aura of grim determination and tight control surrounding him. She rubbed her hand down the front pleat of her skirt to keep from reaching over and smoothing his wrinkles, kissing his lips until they smiled, dispelling his dark mood.

But her eyes involuntarily clung to his hard, unyielding mouth. Those taut lips would soften, yield to gentle kisses. They always had. Mark Manchester could be as hard as the nails his men drove into lumber, but with her his tough exterior melted into a honeyed sweetness.

Purposely Sara pinched the side of her leg to draw her attention away from him. Was this another heart-tugging ploy? she wondered, constantly on guard. She doubted it. He wasn't aware of her careful scrutiny.

"Do you want to go to the Bishops' party tomorrow night?" she asked, knowing that Mark had avoided "teacher get-togethers" in the past. No doubt he found them boring. But the thought of Mark being jealous of Jared was repugnant to her. She wasn't as uptight as Hal Moran, and yet she found Mark's accusation of her having an affair extremely distasteful. Perhaps if he saw how happy Jared and Beth Ann were, he'd see how bizarre his accusation was.

"Do you really want me to tag along?"

Mark knew how out of place he'd be. Teachers' parties invariably led to shoptalk. The first and last party he'd attended, the men had heatedly discussed positive reinforcement. It sounded like bribery to Mark, but when he had said so, they looked at him as though he'd stepped in from outer space. The male teachers condenscendingly tossed justifiable reward and Skinner's pigeon theory at him. Who the hell was Skinner? And what was a grown man doing playing with pigeons?

"It isn't much fun going alone," Sara replied.

"It isn't much fun being the butt of the jokes, either. I don't have much in common with those guys."

69

"You weren't the butt of anyone's jokes," Sara protested. "Several of the men said you solved some of their handyman problems. They appreciated your help."

Sara realized that Mark felt uncomfortable around teachers but couldn't understand why. By societal standards male teachers were at the bottom of the social scale and contractors were near the top. To her knowledge there wasn't a teacher who didn't admire Mark's business success.

"Would you consider attending a barbecue at Moran's farm next month?" Mark bargained. "It isn't much fun going to builders' social functions alone, either."

Sara could taste the flavor of her own words. To be fair, if she insisted on Mark accompanying her, she couldn't refuse his invitation. She watched his hands tighten on the steering wheel. He expected an argument.

"I'd love to," she said, accepting with a wide grin.

"You would?" Mark took his eyes off the road to see if she was kidding.

"Yes, I would. . . . Mark, you missed our driveway."

The next evening Sara could hear Mark moving around in the room next to hers as they dressed for Jared and Beth Ann's party. She'd changed clothes twice and still wasn't convinced that she qualified in the bells-on-the-toes category.

"Face it," she muttered, "you're acting like a teenager on your first date."

She sorted through her jewelry box, looking for the right accent piece for her pale blue, scoop-necked cocktail dress. Nothing suited it. The necklaces were too heavy, the pins too formal, and the earrings too small. She fingered the dainty diamond earrings Mark had given her on Jamie's first birthday. Too dressy, she decided, lightly twirling the gold post between her thumb and forefinger, mesmerized by the bluish-white glitter reflected from her dress.

A small warmth fluttered in her stomach as she also recalled Mark framing her face with his large hands, then nimbly inserting the diamond posts. Her skin tingled with the remembrance of his lips lightly grazing her forehead, her cheeks, her lips. She'd missed his gentle caresses as much as she'd missed their passionate lovemaking.

Startled, she dropped the earring when she heard a sharp rap on the door, followed by Mark entering the room. "I can't decide what jewelry to wear," she babbled, furious with herself to be caught daydreaming about the physical side of their marriage.

"Try these."

Sara started to protest his giving her another gift. Gifts weren't what she wanted from him. A pink tinge swept over her cheeks. Moments ago she'd wanted his special brand of lovemaking. She certainly couldn't tell him that!

"Thank you," she responded politely as she took a small box from the palm of his hand.

71

"I hope you like them."

Holding his breath, he anxiously watched Sara while she untied the pink ribbon and opened the box. He'd always prided himself in giving her nothing but the best, but when he'd seen these earrings, he hadn't been able to resist buying them.

Sara lifted the cluster of small silver bells that dangled from infinitesimally tiny links of chain. The slightest motion made the miniature clappers chime delightfully.

"They must have been left over from the Christmas selection," Mark apologized. "I asked if they had any in gold—"

Sara interrupted. "They're beautiful. Perfect."

"May I put them on you?" Mark asked, his breath finally released.

Rising, Sara held the dangling bells out to him. Her dark eyelids fluttered closed as she felt his breath fanning over her face. He was close; so close, his warmth seemed to envelop her. Automatic reflexes brought the palms of her hands to the pure whiteness of the front of his shirt. Beneath the silky fabric she could feel his heart race, matching the pace of her own.

"A kiss?" Mark requested when he'd completed his task. "A small kiss for a small gift?" Of love, he silently added, wishing with all his heart that the gift had been of higher quality.

Sara opened her eyes. Both the flash of hunger in her eyes and the harsh rise and fall of his chest could have been a trick of the imagination, it was so brief.

"This is the way it's going to be from now on," Mark promised, patiently waiting for a response. "I'll give; I'll never take."

Never leave me? she silently wondered.

"You can't bargain for affection," she temporized, uncertain that her need for affection from Mark wouldn't take them too far, too fast. The bed they'd shared could easily be reached with three of his long-legged strides. Banish the thought, she thought, mentally chastising herself. He asked for a kiss. Only a kiss. Deep down Sara admitted to herself that she was hungry for more. "A kiss," she whispered lamely.

"Because you want to, not because of the gift?" He had difficulty comprehending getting something with no strings attached. To him gifts were like installment payments that were due with monthly regularity. No gift. No love.

Sara's fingers circled behind the pristine whiteness of his collar. As her head tilted, the tiny bells chimed. She stretched on tiptoe to reach the fullness of his lower lip. She felt his arms hesitantly circle her waist, as though uncertain of their welcome.

Oh, Mark, she whispered silently, *I love you.*

Her parted lips covered his. His lips remained sealed, but pliant, against hers as she tasted him. The tip of her tongue boldly traced the path of the tense white line she'd worried about. Her fingers brushed against his forehead to remove the thin lines of stress. As her hands slid downward she felt a muscle in his jaw pulsate, as though Mark strove to keep tight control over himself.

Sara had little idea how much the kiss cost Mark. He silently struggled to maintain the loose hold when he wanted desperately to pull her tightly against him. Her lips gently encouraged him to take the initiative, to thrust his tongue between her malleable lips, to fully taste her sweetness. He couldn't. The thin thread of control would snap if he did. Within a second he'd be tearing at her dress like an animal, throwing her on the bed, burying himself deep inside of her. He couldn't, but oh, God, how he wanted her.

With a quiet sigh Sara eased away from him, resting her heels on the floor.

"Okay?" Mark whispered, needing reassurance that he hadn't overstepped the boundaries.

"You kept your lips closed," she commented without prior thought.

Mark's eyes glanced at the bed. "We'll be late for the party," he replied, his voice husky from memories of the two of them entwined between the sheets.

The silver bells tinkled as Sara nodded. He was right. Desire wasn't the solution to their problems. He exercised control. Why couldn't she? On a rational level she should have refused even the smallest of kisses. But love, she realized once again, to her chagrin, wasn't rational. Love made the lightest caress a dangerous combination of raw instinct and need.

They left for the party, neither of them in a party mood. Their thoughts lingered on what had

74

and what had not taken place in the master bedroom. Each of them weighed and measured the ecstasy of being reunited against the heavy barriers keeping them apart. As though synchronized by the blind master of fate, their eyes never met, although they frequently glanced with longing at each other.

Parked cars lined both sides of the street in front of the Bishops' house. As Mark searched for a parking place he heard music and laughter coming from the celebration when the door opened and closed. His lips tilted into a half smile as he practiced greeting Sara's teacher friends. The skin across his knuckles stretched tightly

He grimaced silently. Another ordeal where he would stand around looking like a damned uneducated idiot. If he was lucky, perhaps they'd ignore him. His hands clenched the wheel tighter. Lucky, hell, that would be worse. His entire youth had been a mixture of overt disdain and being cruelly ignored. Politely dismissed, Mark predicted, feeling his unworthiness rising to the surface. Carefully he reviewed his plan of action. He'd smile and keep his mouth shut. A grinning idiot? he thought, admonishing himself. Oh, hell, if worse came to worse, he'd ask Jared if there was anything around the house that needed to be repaired.

"There's a place," Sara said, pointing down the street. "Jared must have invited the entire faculty and the administration."

Mark groaned quietly. One wrong word and Sara could lose her job. She'd never forgive him.

He'd be sleeping back at the shop and eating out of cans again.

"Are you as nervous as I am?" Sara asked as Mark parked the car.

He revealed more than intended with his reply. "No reason to be scared spitless."

"My mouth feels like I ate a bowl of cottonballs for dinner too," Sara confessed.

"What are *you* nervous about? These are your friends."

"Friends ask a whole lot of questions I'd rather avoid answering."

Mark picked up her damp hand and wove his fingers between hers. He reassured her when he couldn't reassure himself. "You'll be poised, calm, and serene. You always are."

Nervously giggling, Sara squeezed his hand. "Your image of me should be slightly tarnished after the way I've been yelling the past couple of days."

"Ladies never yell," he teased. "Raise their voices on rare occasions, possibly. But never, ever do they yell."

"On the inside ladies quietly have the screaming meamies," Sara replied.

Mark chuckled. "Almost five years of marriage and I didn't know you were scared of anything." His face sobered. "Guess we've both been wearing a brave mask, haven't we?"

She nodded, and the silver bells tinkled, as though laughing at their unspoken fears. Sara flicked them, listening to their merry sound.

Raising the back of her other hand to his lips,

Mark said, "Stay close to me tonight, please. I'd rather face a room filled with union officials than walk in there."

Sara grinned at the thought of protecting Mark from the teachers. There wasn't a man on the entire faculty who could match his physical appeal, charisma, or worldly experience.

"I'll stay close," she vowed, secretly thrilled at the prospect of having an excuse to play the role of being happily married.

At the brightly lit front door Jared and Beth Ann greeted them warmly.

"Mark, welcome. We're glad you could come." Beth Ann grinned from ear to ear as she said impishly, "I understand that you caught Jared making a pass at your wife."

"Darling," Jared protested when Mark's expression became grim. "Don't you find it difficult to walk around with your feet in your mouth?"

"Small feet, big mouth?" Beth Ann quipped, wrapping one arm around Mark's waist and the other around Sara's. Her dark eyes rolled toward the ceiling. "Twenty-five years and he still tells me *everything.*"

Jared laughed, poking fun at himself. "Sounds like I'm the one with the big mouth, doesn't it?"

"With those size twelves of his he never goes hungry," Beth Ann said, continuing to tease. "Mark, I think you've met everyone here." Her voice dropped to a confidential low pitch. "Beware. They've all brought their list of mechanical problems. Be certain to stay away from Jennifer Blalock. Her foundation is cracked."

"That isn't all that will be cracked if she latches on to Mark," Sara whispered, glancing at the well-stacked redhead who was smiling at the football coach.

"Jealous?" Mark asked, smiling. As Beth Ann stepped from between them he whispered for Sara's ears alone, "A little green monster hidden in there with the screaming meamies? I'm learning a lot about my teacher-wife, aren't I?"

"Careful, Mr. Manchester," she warned half seriously. "There are other things inside of me I won't reveal if I catch you fixing . . . foundations."

Mark's smile reflected his deep satisfaction at her reply. "Sweetheart, I don't know a thing about pouring concrete. I'm concentrating my efforts on constructing a bell tower for a certain belle."

Her earrings saucily chimed as she shook her head to clear the image of being isolated with Mark in a tower high above and far away from the past. His eyes held mirth, but the laughter covered something more. She ducked her head, realizing that her eyes could be revealing the part of her that was his alone. "We'd better mix and mingle."

His hand slid to the back of her waist as he bent down and nuzzled the sensitive place the bells lightly touched. "I'm going to enjoy this party."

Sara knew what he meant. The teachers knew that she and Mark had recently reconciled. They expected to see loving gestures exchanged between Mark and herself. Smiling and temporarily setting their problems aside, she responded by brushing her hand across his smoothly shaven jaw. "Me too."

Beth Ann hadn't been kidding. For the next two hours Sara cuddled against Mark while he gave tips on fixing everything from broken clay roof tiles to creaking floor joists. Most of the time she didn't have the vaguest idea what Mark prescribed. His hand teased the side of her waist, reminding her that his thoughts were never far from her.

The party drew to a close after Jared and Beth Ann cut a replica of their wedding cake and fed each other small bites. Beth Ann laughed at the wrong time. Frothy white icing clung to the corner of her mouth. With abandoned glee Jared proceeded to clean her up with loud, smacking kisses.

A jarring note threatened to end the festivities when a math teacher Sara barely knew began weaving toward the door.

"Jist git me to my car. I'll be all right," Mark heard him slur.

Sara watched a pained expression cross Mark's face. In a moment of complete understanding their eyes locked. Mark excused himself.

"Hey, Todd," Mark said, slapping the math teacher on the back in a friendly manner. "Didn't you say you live in the Blackhawk subdivision?"

"Yeah." His laughter raised to a high pitch as he leaned heavily against Mark. "You built 'em, didn't ya?"

"You know, it's been a long time since I've

been over there. How about letting me drive you home?"

"Naw, it's too dark to see anything. I can make it."

"Those floodlights on the main gate still causing problems?"

"Floodlights?"

It was apparent to Sara and everyone watching that Todd was inebriated. Mark handled Todd in a diplomatic manner, but Sara wanted to give Todd a tongue-lashing and grab the keys he jangled in front of Mark's face.

"The ones in the bushes. My office had a call about replacing them. I'd consider it a favor if I could drive you home and check them out."

"A favor? Well, ol' buddy, you did a fine job on my house. The least I can do is give ya a ride."

Mark plucked the keys from Todd's hand as he guided him through the door.

" 'Night, everybody!" Todd yelled loudly.

Sara gathered her purse from the bedroom, bid Beth Ann and Jared a quick good-bye, then rushed to her car. Todd weaved from one side of the sidewalk to the other as Mark tried to keep him from falling.

As she followed the late-model sedan that Mark drove, she wiped away an angry tear trickling down her cheek. The spring air held a long-remembered chill. This could have been another night, another drunk. Todd could have been behind the wheel causing an accident.

"Oh, Mark," she whispered, "thank God you were there."

80

CHAPTER FIVE

"Todd wanted to drive himself home, didn't he?" Sara asked the minute Mark backed out of Todd's driveway.

"Yes."

The silver bells tinkled as Sara sadly shook her head. "He could have—"

"He didn't," Mark interrupted, following her train of thought. "Don't think about it."

"Don't think about it? How do I stop thinking about it? If you hadn't been there and insisted on driving, that . . . *drunk* would have been behind the wheel."

"If I hadn't done it, someone else would have," he said tersely. Mark furtively glanced at Sara, mentally cursing Todd for ruining the closeness that had begun to develop between Sara and himself.

Sara realized that ranting and raving at Mark was inexcusable. No one person could monitor how much a stranger imbibed or could be held responsible for keeping them off the roads.

"I have to call Jared tomorrow morning," Mark said, hoping to divert Sara from silently slipping back into the past.

"I'll send them a bread-and-butter note thanking them for inviting us to their party."

"I'm supposed to call him if you object to he and I playing tennis tomorrow morning."

Sara straightened. "Tennis? Tomorrow is Saturday. Don't you have to go into the shop to do the books?"

"While you were at your meeting last night I went to the shop and took care of it. What kind of tennis player is Jared?"

"Wicked serve. Lousy backhand," Sara replied. "His teenage daughter, Libby, clobbers him regularly."

Mark chuckled. "From what I saw tonight I'd bet Libby isn't the only one clobbering him. Beth Ann's tongue wields a wicked serve too."

"She isn't exactly a retiring housewife, is she? She keeps him on his toes." Sara smiled. "Jared would be lost without her."

"I know that feeling," Mark confessed as he raised his arm to the back of Sara's seat. But he didn't allow himself to touch Sara, to draw her close to his side.

"You and Jared are as different as day and night." Sara desperately wanted to feel his callused hand massage the back of her neck to relieve the tension Todd had induced with his drunkenness.

"How so?"

"Psychologists have all the right questions. You have the answers. Jared would have sobered Todd up by drilling him with a thousand questions. You're a man of action. You kept him from behind the wheel by taking him home."

Her head brushed his forearm as she sank back against the headrest. Sara closed her eyes.

"Was that a compliment?" Mark clenched his hand to keep it from threading through the silkiness of her hair.

"I guess it was," Sara murmured, turning her head toward him. "You're a good man, Mark."

Good? Mark withdrew his arm and put both hands on the steering wheel, wondering if the cups of fruit punch Sara had been drinking were spiked with alcohol. His thoughts at the moment were anything other than pure and innocent, and miles away from being good. All he wanted to do was make love to her until they were exhausted.

"Why did you move your arm?" Sara asked.

"We're nearly home."

She squeezed her eyes tightly closed until floating dots blurred the glaring connection between touching her and being home. The party pretense of being reunited lingered, but it was drawing swiftly to an end. She turned her head toward the window and peered into the darkness. They were less than a block from the house.

Mark cast a quick glance at her and saw her facial muscles tense. "Don't get uptight."

"Should I be uptight?" she countered wistfully.
"No."

Mark pulled into the driveway and turned the key. Moonlight filtering through the budding leaves of the pecan tree beside the drive softly highlighted Sara's fragileness. The shadow of the tree trunk cloaked the rounded thrust of her breasts in velvet darkness. He didn't need light to imagine how her breasts filled his hands.

A dark kind of pain washed over his face. "We'd better go in."

Sara crossed her arms over her chest and rubbed her forearms. The thought of going inside, climbing the steps, listening to Mark undress and go to bed alone brought a deep sigh to Sara's lips. Living without Mark had been like going from bright sunlight to darkness, but living with him made the darkness miserably cold.

"I think I'll sit on the porch for a while."

"You're shivering right now." Mark got out, went around the car, opened her door, and quickly shed his suit jacket. "If you insist on sitting on the back porch, then wear my jacket."

Lethargically Sara swung her feet to the pavement and slowly stood. Mark settled his jacket on her shoulders. The sensation of being snuggly enveloped by the warmth of his body heat and the fragrance of his masculine cologne brought a shimmer of mist to her eyes.

The party's over, she reminded herself as she pulled the lapels closer.

"I'll sit with you," Mark offered. Standing behind her, he smoothed the arms of the jacket against her arms. Any excuse to touch her was valid. "I wouldn't want you falling asleep in the swing again."

Sara automatically laughed. How many times had he accused her of being like a cat lazily curled up on the porch swing, drifting off to sleep?

"I'm awake. You can go . . ." To bed, she almost said but substituted, "Inside."

"Are you trying to get rid of me?" Mark cupped her elbow as they climbed the steep back steps to the screened-in porch.

Flustered by the underlying meaning beneath his question, she simply shook her head. The silver bells tinkled her reply.

Mark held the screen door open, then followed her. "Avoiding being alone with me?"

Alone with myself is better than being alone with you, she started to reply but bit back the honest response. "With an early tennis match in the morning I thought you'd need some sleep."

Mark snorted. "Sweetheart, going to bed doesn't insure sleep. Can't you hear me tossing and turning?"

"The walls in these old houses are thick." The wooden swing squeaked as she sat down to relieve her shaky knees. Last night she'd purposely arrived home after midnight to avoid the pangs of seeing him go into the spare bedroom. Bone-tired, she'd gone to bed, but sleep had evaded her. "I must have zonked out immediately," she prevaricated, unwilling to admit that she hadn't slept a wink.

"The sleep of the innocent. How I envy you."

Mark sat on the opposite side of the swing. He slowly rocked the swing back and forth. The soothing motion lessened his driving need for Sara. He loosened his tie, opened a couple of buttons on his shirt. "Want a cup of coffee?"

"Do you?"

"No. Caffeine won't help me sleep."

Through half closed lids Sara peeked at Mark. His strong fingers were laced behind his head. His broad shoulders stretched his shirt across his chest. The moon shed enough light for her to see the thick mat of hair the white shirt accented. Her hands clutched the lapels against her throat as her eyes continued to stray. His slacks hugged his muscular thighs, which were parted in his relaxed pose.

"Don't look at me with those sleepy bedroom eyes," Mark whispered. Her secretive, shy glance raced across his flesh as though they were gentle probes bringing him to life. "You know I want to sleep with you."

Caught staring, Sara felt her cheeks flame. "Sleeping together wouldn't solve our problems."

"It would solve one of mine," he quipped, turning toward her. "I hate sleeping alone."

Even in the darkness his blue eyes blazed with hunger. His arms dropped to his side and he leaned inches closer. A familiar stirring warned Sara to be cautious. She lowered her eyes to keep him from seeing the love shining in her eyes.

"Honest talk. Isn't that what you wanted?" He

placed his hand over her fist, drawing his jacket higher to her throat.

"Don't. I can't think straight when you touch me."

"I don't want you to think straight. I want you to feel, to remember how good we are together."

"Mark," she said, protesting and refusing to loosen her grip on his jacket. "We can't just . . ."

"Go to bed? Make love? We're married. Why can't we?"

"It's too easy."

Mark pushed himself from the swing and strode to the screen overlooking the backyard. "Easy? Dammit, I'm in a dog-eat-dog world all day. I'd appreciate not having to fight for bedroom privileges at night."

"Then don't." Sara's temper flared. The swing hit the wall as she jumped to her feet. "Find yourself a new home with a new bedroom!"

"I don't want a new home or a new wife, dammit! I want you!" He pivoted around. In a hushed voice he demanded, "Look at me, Sara. All evening you've teased and tormented me by brushing up against me, holding my arm so it touched your breasts, leaning forward until your neckline gapped. Admit it."

"I wasn't teasing you."

"What do you call those smiling promises you made?" Mark advanced toward her.

Sara stepped back until her shoulders touched the wall. "I'll admit to flirting with you."

Mark plowed his fingers through his hair in

frustration. "If that stupid fool hadn't gotten drunk, you'd be wrapped around me, shouting my name in ecstasy rather than arguing with me on the porch. Well, sweetheart, you wanted me hot and bothered. For what it's worth, congratulations. You succeeded."

"I made it perfectly clear the night you came back that we're going to—you couldn't—" Sara stammered as she fought desire and spoke at the same time. She'd always been a terrible liar.

His hands blocked her attempt to end the argument by fleeing into the house as they landed on either side of her shoulders. "What? Make love with me? Quit politely tiptoeing around the issue. Say it!"

"I'm not going to make love with you," she stated without hesitation. "I apologize if I mistakenly led you to believe that after one pleasant evening together I would forgive and forget."

She pushed against his forearm. His elbow locked, continuing to bar her from leaving.

"You aren't going anywhere."

"I'd like to go inside. I'm cold."

Harsh laughter burst through his lips. "Another subtle invitation?"

"No. Statement of fact."

"I'm into fact-finding. Tell me, sweetheart, how long? How long am I sentenced to sleeping in the spare room?" His hips cradled against hers. "How long are you going to tempt me, then deny me the pleasures we *both* want?"

Sara kept her head averted until she felt his lips string a path of hot kisses from her ear to the sensitive hollow of her collarbone. Her knees threatened to buckle as he sensuously rotated his hips, unashamed of the arousal she'd caused.

"I want to feel myself inside you," he hoarsely whispered, losing control. "That's my home. I want to be part of you."

Struggling to keep her balance, her hands reflexively clung to his belt.

"Yes, sweetheart, please, please touch me. Take me home."

His lips opened over hers. With one masterful stroke his tongue filled her. No! her mind screamed. She was making the same foolish mistake! She was letting passion take control. His tongue dipped and swirled, banishing her cool reason, throwing her logic carelessly into the fragrant spring air.

Her arms tightened around his back. She returned his kiss, sucking him deep inside, darting her tongue rapidly between his teeth. A small groan from the back of her throat signaled her submission. One of his hands raised the hem of her dress, touching her firm buttocks, rolling her panty hose and bikini briefs downward, while the other tugged at her zipper. His jacket slipped from her shoulders.

Sara hastily unbuttoned his shirt, eager to feel her taut breasts against the supple warmth of his skin. She shrugged her shoulders when she felt the zipper give to allow the dress to fall. With agile fingers Mark unsnapped the back fastening of her lacy bra. That, too, Sara shrugged off.

Clothed only in moonlight from the waist up,

Mark closed his hand over her breasts, roughly massaging them until the dusky nipples puckered between his fingers.

"Oh, sweetheart, I promised I wouldn't take." He raised his head until his eyes locked with hers. The calluses on his palms raked against her sensitized nipples. "Each step of the way you're going to have to ask." His voice shook with emotion, but Mark didn't care.

"Kiss me there," Sara responded, arching the fullness of her breasts against his palm. She felt him fondle her, teasing her, but his eyes didn't waver. "Do I have to beg?"

"Would you?" His thumb and forefinger pinched lightly. "Shhh, I don't want you to beg. Beggars have no pride."

He inched away from her. Starved though he was for their lovemaking, he wouldn't take her like an animal with her back pinned against the wall. He lifted her into his arms, carrying her into their home.

"Don't have second thoughts, sweetheart," he whispered, capturing her lips as he strode through the darkness.

Feeling weightless in his muscular arms, Sara thought of nothing other than the urgency strumming rampantly through her body. She twined her fingers in his hair, impatiently tugging, communicating her desire to Mark with the flicking of her tongue along his ear.

During their separation she'd forbidden herself from remembering how his touch, his softly spoken words of love made life's harsh realities fade into insignificance. Bones of contention became moot.

Mark Manchester, her husband, her love, was her reason for living.

There were other causes she'd fought for and against. She believed in fairness and equality. She'd marched for women's rights. She'd campaigned for political candidates. She championed those less fortunate than herself. But for now, high, lofty ideals sealed themselves in an ivory tower.

Her entire being responded to one cause: Mark.

Her head spun as he laid her on the eiderdown comforter and peeled off the rest of his clothes. A moment later he pulled her into his arms.

"Sweetheart, hold me. Don't let me go."

"I'll never let you go," she vowed, embracing him with equal fervor. Her fingers curled into the muscles of his back with a strength of one possessed. Her long, polished nails raked his back as her deepest fear was exposed. *"Don't leave me!"* she whispered, a flash of anguish making her rigid.

His arms tightened around her until they were suffocatingly close. "The good part of me never left, love, only the animal."

Sara wasn't certain she understood his meaning. Ripples of pleasure pulsed through her as he molded her breasts against his face. Stubbles of his dark whiskers lightly abraded the tender globes. His breath brought the tips to aching hardness. Anticipation of the magical delights she knew him capable of made her arch toward him.

"Make love to me," she encouraged.

"You're the only sane thing in my life." Mark didn't know if he said the words or merely thought them, but he knew they were true. "You make me clean. I'm nothing without you, Sara. I need you."

Sara felt his lips moving against her breasts, but, caught in the web of passion, she couldn't decipher what she heard. Her blood pounded in her ears; her lips chanted his name. Her physical longing narrowed to the thin line between pleasure and pain.

"Love me, Mark. Don't make me wait any longer."

"Take me home, sweetheart, take me home."

Her hand guided him, welcoming him home to the sweet intimacy of love.

Mark wrapped her legs around his hips to bind them closer. Arms braced, he clenched his teeth to keep from telling her what her innocent loving meant to a man who was a product of the slums. He sheltered her from the truth with the same compassion that granted him shelter deep within her. This primitive, age-old ritual between husband and wife strengthened his resolve to remain silent. He'd be banned forever if she knew who and what he had been.

Sara drew a shaky breath. Her nails left tracks on his shoulders. Colors collided. She arched. He thrust. They catapulted into their own private world that held no past, no future, only the satiating present.

Set adrift in time, Sara relaxed. She heard Mark's breathing slowly return to a normal rate that matched hers, but she wanted to continue drifting in this safe realm where reality couldn't disturb her.

"Go to sleep, sweetheart," Mark whispered in her ear. "I'm here beside you."

The reassurance that this wasn't a beautiful dream permitted Sara to obey. He'd be there. Her lips barely tilted upward. She curled against him as he pulled the sheet over them. He'd be there.

The abysmal loneliness had ended.

CHAPTER SIX

"I'm coming," Mark muttered under his breath, taking one last look at Sara as she slept. Throughout the night she'd clung to him. A tender smile of satisfaction mingled with his desire to climb back in bed and let Jared Bishop find another tennis partner.

The pounding on the back screen door continued.

Hastily Mark dashed into the spare bedroom for his tennis shorts and shirt, then rushed down the steps. "Just a minute!"

Jared grinned at Beth Ann and pointed to the clothing strewn on the floor of the porch. "Told you we should have gone to the front door."

"Shame on you! Sara is probably airing them. You know how smoke at a party permeates everything." Beth Ann kept a straight face, but her

94

eyes danced merrily. "I aired my clothes on the staircase."

Chuckling, Jared hugged his wife. "Is that what you call the brazen way you lured me to the bedroom?"

"Me? Brazen? You aired your clothes in the hallway. You didn't make it to the stairs."

"You attacked me, as I recall." A smug smile wreathed his face.

Beth Ann tapped him playfully on his temple with her forefinger. "Old age is making your mind fuzzy. Weren't you the one—"

"Is this a private argument or can anyone join in?" Mark asked, opening the screen door.

"We were discussing the merits of the Kinsey Report," Beth Ann quipped. She glanced at Jared as though he were an expert on the sexual revolution of the sixties. "Isn't he the one who had the beans-in-the-jar theory?"

Jared's face turned bright red.

"Experimental psychology this early?" Mark teased, ushering them toward the kitchen as he nonchalantly gathered the discarded clothing and tossed it into the laundry room. When he noticed the knowing smiles on their faces, he grinned. "Guess we missed the clothes hamper."

Beth Ann nudged Jared in the ribs. "But not the bean jar."

Quizzically Mark glanced from Beth Ann to Jared.

"Tell him," Jared mumbled. "Otherwise he'll make reference to it throughout the tennis match to throw me off my game."

95

Batting her eyes with feigned innocence, Beth Ann seated herself at the kitchen table. "Never mind," she said tormentingly. "I'd hate to attribute *your* theory to a famous sexologist."

Mark's ears perked up. "Oh, *that* Kinsey. Don't tell me he raised pigeons too."

Rubbing her full lower lip, Beth Ann quipped, "Rabbits were more his style."

Despite himself, Jared chuckled. "You're outrageously disrespectful."

"And you love it," his wife replied saucily. "I'll bet Sara's bean jar would have been empty years ago."

"You're determined to undermine my tennis game, aren't you?" Jared moved behind his wife and rested his hands on her shoulders. Leaning forward, he playfully circled her neck with his thumbs at the back of her neck, his fingers on her slender throat. In a villainous stage whisper he commanded, "Tell him before he dies of curiosity and you're executed for revealing classified research information."

Beth Ann blithely removed his stranglehold, then kissed the palms of each of his hands. "Well, love, if you insist." Her voice dropped to a confidential tone. "On our honeymoon I found a bag of coffee beans and a jar tucked away in Jared's suitcase. Naturally, being inquisitive by nature, I asked if Jared was researching a new birth-control device."

Mark's dark eyebrows rose as he seated himself directly across the table from Beth Ann.

Interrupting his wife, Jared explained, "One of

her zany college roommates told Beth Ann that aspirin was an effective means of birth control . . . when held tightly between her knees."

Cocking her head upward, she countered, "His *brainy* college roommate recommended orange juice. Every time you get the urge, you wait for a can of frozen orange juice to melt. By that time the urge goes away."

Mark grinned. Either of their methods would have been more effective than the drugstore contraceptive he had used with Sara.

"Neither aspirin nor orange juice prevented conception of our two darling offspring. But that's another story—back to the bean theory." Beth Ann took a quick breath. Her eyes twinkled with merriment. "My scholarly husband hypothesized that if you drop a bean in the jar every time you make love during the first year, then take a bean out every time you make love the second year, you'll never remove all the beans during the rest of your marriage."

Mark glanced from Beth Ann to Jared, tempted to ask the inevitable question. He didn't know Beth Ann well, but he felt certain that the information would be volunteered.

"Ours is half empty or half full, depending upon how you evaluate the data." Beth Ann playfully elbowed Jared in the ribs. "Jared drank buckets of orange juice the first year we were married, so I think he invalidated his own hypothesis."

Dropping a kiss on his wife's head, Jared

winked at Mark. "She wanted to name our first child Bayer."

"That's better than Sunkist!" Mark teased, his deep laughter joining Beth Ann's infectious giggles.

Upstairs, the sound of their voices awakened Sara, and the giddy laughter she heard made her hastily climb from the warm cocoon of the bed, rush to the bathroom, splash cold water on her face, and throw on a pair of jeans and a loose sweatshirt. Two minutes later she pushed the swinging kitchen door open. "What's going on here?"

Rising to his feet, Mark wiped his eyes and gestured for her to sit down. "Jared and Beth Ann were explaining a couple of their research projects."

"You're the one who needs the chair. You'd better sit down before you fall down," Sara instructed as she watched Mark hold his ribs and gasp for breath between bursts of laughter. "I'll fix the coffee."

"Coffee?" Beth Ann hooted. "Ground from fresh beans?"

As though on cue, all three of them bent at the waist in a new fit of laughter. Sara didn't know what the joke was about, but she couldn't keep from smiling as Beth Ann tried to recap the gist of the conversation.

Laughter, she mused, was one of the missing ingredients essential in the recipe for marriage she and Mark had followed. They'd both been, as the kids at school would say, too intense, too uptight. Jamie, with his antics typical of a four-year-old, had been the comic relief in their marriage.

A circle of sharp pain centered in her chest. Jamie wasn't here to keep them laughing.

Go with the flow, she instructed herself, taking another page from the teenager's philosophy book.

After measuring coffee into a filter and pouring water into the percolator, Sara crossed to the cabinet for cups and saucers. The boisterous laughter quietly died to mere chuckles when Beth Ann finished her version of what had been said prior to Sara's arrival in the kitchen.

Determined not to spoil the congeniality, Sara placed the sugar bowl in front of Jared, saying, "Shall I pour you a cup? Or would you rather eliminate the middle man and drink yours out of the sugar bowl?"

Jared pushed the sugar toward his wife, crowing, "If you think I oversweeten my coffee, watch Beth Ann."

"That's why we're such a sweet couple," Beth Ann responded merrily. "Jared has a theory about coffee drinkers too."

"Enough," Jared pleaded. "Let's leave a few dark secrets for Mark to discover. You've already convinced him I sit around in my office dreaming up cockeyed ideas. My image is ruined."

"Tarnished, love," Beth Ann said, correcting him. "Just enough to keep you interesting. I'll wager that Sara drinks hers strong and dark. . . . Mark will add a touch of cream and sugar."

As Sara placed a cup of aromatic brew in front of Mark, his arm snaked around her waist and pulled her onto his lap. "We should blow his theory by drinking warm Coke. He'd have a heck of a time figuring that out, wouldn't he?"

Sara nodded. "You'd lose your wager, Beth Ann. Mark and I drink ours black."

"Are you a gambling man?" Jared asked Mark, to divert the discussion away from his wacky theories.

"Depends on the wager and what's being gambled," Mark said, hedging. Sara squirmed, nestling closer, wrapping her arm around his shoulder. Mark shifted her toward his knees as a sharp pang of desire blazed. Mark considered forfeiting the tennis match in favor of an extended game of mattress polo. In that game he didn't care who came out on top.

Jared stuck his hand forward. "I'll bet a dinner at our house that I can beat you on the tennis court."

Before Mark could reply, Beth Ann grabbed her husband's hand. "Now wait a minute. Who's doing the cooking?" She glanced at Sara and grimaced. "Why is it that men play games and their wives are stuck with the chores? Sara and I will go play. You guys slave away over the kitchen stove for a change."

Somewhat prepared for another round of prolonged banter that was about to take place between Sara's friends, Mark injected, "How about all of us playing tennis, then coming back here

100

and fixing Chinese food? I'm not great on the tennis court, but I wield a mean wok."

"Beth Ann swore off tennis years ago when I refused to let her win," Jared said. The smug, superior smile on his face begged for another sharp retort from his wife.

"Keep your mouth rolling, champ, and you'll be eating beans for dinner—coffee beans," Beth Ann promised, winking at Sara. "I came over for a friendly chat. You know my idea of exercising is eating a doughnut and seeing how fast I can talk to burn off the calories."

"In that case, let's gulp down a cup of coffee and head for the courts." Mark couldn't resist letting his hand stray from Sara's waist to her knee as he felt her shift to rise. "Want to watch?" he asked her.

Beth Ann giggled. "Don't mind us. I told Jared you'd want to be alone, but he insisted on speeding over here this morning."

"You told me to hurry," Jared retorted.

"You're confused. Last night when you were emptying ashtrays, I told you to hurry to bed." Beth Ann flashed Mark and Sara a cheeky grin. "I'm certain—well, almost certain—that I told him to slow down. Then again, maybe it was last night after he came to bed that I told him to slow down, and this morning—"

"Never mind, Beth Ann," Sara said, rising and turning toward her guests but standing close enough to brush against Mark as he rose to his feet. "I have a feeling that Beth Ann is going to

101

get enough exercise to drop from a size ten to a size five before the tennis match is over."

Mark squeezed her waist, reluctant to leave the house but anxious to get back from playing tennis to be with Sara. Why had he volunteered to fix dinner for them? Purely selfish, protective instincts, he realized. Sara wouldn't berate him for what happened last night in front of her friends. And, after attending the Bishops' party, he knew Beth Ann's open-mouth-insert-foot monologue would keep Sara from morosely dwelling on what she should have done to avoid sharing the king-size bed.

"We won't be gone long," Mark promised, stealing a quick kiss from Sara's upturned lips.

"Take your time, gentlemen. If Sara gets tired of listening to me, we'll go to the mall and spend some of your hard-earned money." Beth Ann grinned wickedly at Jared, then met him halfway across the table for a kiss. "Don't let the thought of my emptying the bank account affect your game."

Jared groaned audibly and crossed to the back door. "She really hates to see me clobber my opponents."

"The checkbook is on the dresser if you need it," Mark said. "Got a theory about that, Jared?"

"Sure do. Contractors make more money than teachers." Jared followed Mark through the screen door.

Sara heard Mark reply, "Teachers have a security factor that contractors envy. They never have to worry about interest rates, building start-ups,

capital expenditures, or the rising cost of labor."
His voice faded as they descended the steps.

"Sounds scary to be in business for yourself,"
Beth Ann commented.

"I don't think Mark knows the meaning of the
word *scared*. In fact, this is the first time I've heard
him mention the pitfalls of being in business for
himself."

Sara sat down across the table from Beth Ann.
Thoughtfully she stirred her coffee. Had the
slowdown in the economy drastically effected
Mark's company? He'd mentioned working in a
dog-eat-dog world, but prior to that he'd always
kept shoptalk separate from family matters. She
really couldn't answer the question. From all out-
ward appearances his business was thriving. Even
when Mark had left her, he'd never been stingy
with money.

Beth Ann clicked her fingers to gain Sara's attention. "Wow! Last night left you in a daze,
didn't it?"

"Your party was great," Sara replied, avoiding
the meaning behind the question.

"Come on, Sara. Jared mutters about professional confidentiality every time I ask him about
you and Mark. It's enough to make a normal wife
jealous."

"You? Jealous? Quit pulling my leg."

Beth Ann sipped her coffee, then grinned. "I
said 'normal wife.' Five years ago, if you remember, I was a typical housewife—if there is such an
animal. And, believe it or not, I found my marriage in trouble."

"That's hard to believe. You and Jared are a perfect couple."

"False impressions. Think back to last night. Did you notice anything missing from the usual anniversary celebration?"

Sara searched her memory, trying to pinpoint anything irregular, but couldn't.

"What does the happy couple usually do after they exchange bites of cake?" Beth Ann prompted. "Don't they sip champagne from each other's glasses?"

"Sometimes. But, to my recollection, neither of you drink." Hard as she tried, Sara couldn't make a connection.

"I'm an alcoholic." Beth Ann leaned back in her chair as though to give Sara breathing space. "Believe me, five years ago I worked hard to create the false impression of being sober."

Slowly Sara rose to her feet and moved toward the coffeepot sitting on the warmer. "I never would have suspected."

"Jared didn't, either. Closet drinkers spend their sober hours thinking up acceptable excuses for their drinking and ways to hide being inebriated."

"How did he find out?" Sara braced herself against the countertop, tempted to cover her ears childishly with her hands.

"He picked me up at the police station in Clayton. DWI."

Sara resisted the urge to wring her hands in consternation. Surely Beth Ann, her friend, realized that she was the last person in the world she should be revealing her circumstances to. Sara hadn't made any pretense about her participation in MADD. For heaven's sake, Beth Ann's signature was on one of the petitions!

"Why are you telling me this? I'd never have found out—"

"Right. And I'd be forced to continue playing the clown to keep our friendship. Sara, when the greasepaint is removed, I'm one scared lady. I couldn't face you after the accident because I thought you'd take one look at me and know that it could have been me behind the wheel."

"It wasn't." Sara refilled both cups and returned to her seat.

"No, I didn't kill anyone, but I don't kid myself into believing it couldn't have happened." Beth Ann stared directly into Sara's eyes. "Do you hate me the way you hate the driver of the car who killed Jamie?"

"I don't . . . ." Sara paused. "You're my friend, Beth Ann. I hate drunk drivers. I'd lock them up and throw away the key if it were in my power." Her shoulders sagged, but her eyes remained steadily on Beth Ann. "But I don't hate you. I know I'd fight to keep you out of jail." Her values in direct conflict, she rubbed her forehead as though by doing so, the conflict would be erased. "Why?"

"Because you care for me. You don't know the man who killed Jamie." Beth Ann paused, noticing the paper napkin she'd shredded into long, thin strips. "I do."

Sara raised her hands, fingers splayed. "Don't tell me about him."

"I have to. You see, he's my friend too."

"You said you value our friendship. Don't say anything more about him."

"He's sick."

"Good! I hope he dies and rots in hell!"

"He'd like you to come to the hospital so he can—"

Sara stood, horrified at the prospect of what she'd say to the man. The chair keeled over behind her, slamming against the floor.

"No!"

Beth Ann sighed heavily. "I had to ask."

"And I have to refuse. I can't forgive him! He took more than an innocent child's life. There's something you don't know about my marriage. I was pregnant with Jamie *before* the ceremony!"

"So what?"

"Mark wouldn't have married me, that's what. Jamie was the slender thread of love binding Mark and I together."

Rising from the chair, Beth Ann circled the table, picked up the chair, and neatly slid it into place. "You're blind, Sara. Hatred keeps you from seeing the driver of the car as a fallible human being, and moral hang-ups keep you from seeing the love that's apparent to anyone who watches Mark."

"Another case study in false impressions. Love didn't enter into the reasoning behind Mark's return. I'm a pawn in a business merger."

"But, I thought . . . I'm certain—"

Sara laughed harshly. "False impressions."

Putting her hand to her forehead, Beth Ann muttered, "If I weren't an alcoholic, I'd seriously consider having a good stiff belt."

Afraid that there was an element of truth in what she heard, Sara wrapped her arm around her friend's shoulder. "I love him. I'm going to teach him to love the woman I've become under his tutelage."

"Sort of a one-woman crusade?" Beth Ann asked, admiring her determination.

"I can't think of a worthier cause, can you?"

"No. I may tease Jared unmercifully, but I fought tooth and nail to kick the habit when I knew I was losing him. Can I do anything to help?" Her irrepressible grin back in place, she suggested, "Maybe we should go shopping and buy you some sexy lingerie."

"I thought the way to a man's heart was through his stomach," Sara quipped.

"Well, lady, get Mark's checkbook. We'll go to the lingerie department of Stix, Bauer, and Fuller, and then we'll stop at Schnuck's. Nothing like covering all the bases."

Later, as they stopped at the grocery store, Sara stopped Beth Ann's chatter long enough to thank her for sharing confidences. She knew it had been extremely difficult under the circumstances to admit to being an alcoholic with a DWI on her driver's license.

"I should have told you when I was having the

problem, but I was too ashamed," Beth Ann replied.

Sara pushed the cart into the checkout lane. "You didn't have anything to be ashamed of. Alcoholism is a sickness."

"When you really believe that, you'll reconsider seeing my friend from Alcoholics Anonymous. He's sick too."

"I'll think about it, Beth Ann," she murmured. "I promise."

CHAPTER SEVEN

At midnight Sara and Mark stood on the front porch waving good-bye as Jared and Beth Ann got into their car.

"Fun day?" Mark asked.

"One of the best."

"Jared is a hell of an athlete. Great sense of balance and timing."

"According to him, he had you running all over the back of the tennis court. As competitive as you are, I'm surprised you spoke to him during dinner."

Mark shut the door. "Games between friends aren't meant to be bloodthirsty."

"Only business is a cutthroat proposition?"

"Let's put it this way: If the success or failure of a project depended on the results of a tennis match, I'd have a severe case of tennis elbow—from practicing day and night before the match."

Sara lazily strolled into the kitchen. Pots, pans, and dishes the men had used to prepare the beef-and-broccoli dish were piled high on the counters. Replete from the dinner and lighthearted conversation, she couldn't have felt less like spending the next hour with dish detergent up to her elbows.

"Why don't we leave them until tomorrow morning?" Mark suggested.

"Yuck. I'd sleep forever with the prospect of facing this mess. Dinner was superb, but you guys used every cooking utensil in the kitchen."

"Gourmet geniuses at work aren't concerned with mundane concerns like dirty dishes."

"Hmm," she answered noncommittally. "You were full of surprises today. I didn't know you played tennis or could cook."

"I recall fixing several breakfasts for you." His arms circled her waist as she squirted soap into the sink.

"Cereal, toast, orange marmalade." Sara invited the strings of kisses he placed down the side of her neck by leaning back against him.

"Sounds like a gourmet breakfast to me."

"How would I know? The breakfast went on the night table." A rush of desire threatened to buckle her knees. His tongue laved the lobe of her ear. In a breathy voice she continued, "And by the time I got around to eating the cereal, it was soggy, and the toast was cold."

Mark grinned at the accuracy of her memory.

"I repeat. Sounds like a gourmet breakfast to me."

"Mmm. The dishes . . . you're distracting me."

He lazily rotated his hips against her and lightly blew a circular pattern from behind her ear to the sensitive hollow of her collarbone. A shiver of delight followed the path of his lips.

"I'll do the dishes in the morning. Let's go to bed," Mark said, tempting her by lightly brushing the budding nipple straining against her shirt. He reached into the sink, pulled the drain stopper, and turned the water off. "I'll share my Chinese fruit-fritter recipe with you on the way up the stairs."

Sara wiped her hands on the dishcloth by the sink.

"I'll have to think of something equally delectable to share with you."

"Oh, sweetheart, tasting you is better than any dessert."

Turning, putting her hands behind his neck, Sara matched his swaying hip motions. "Could we postpone the Chinese cooking lesson until later?"

"Indefinitely." Mark bent and lithely lifted her into his arms.

"Carrying me up the steps is becoming a habit," Sara said, tracing his ear with the tip of her finger.

"Like it? I had the impression that you liked getting everywhere under your own power."

"Even independent women enjoy masterful men on some occasions," she crooned.

Mark mounted the steps with ease, raising her high against his powerful chest to avoid bumping her legs on the banister.

"You're breathing hard. Put me down."

"My breathing has nothing to do with carrying you." He grinned wryly. "Well, maybe it does. But it doesn't have anything to do with how much you weigh. I've carried two-by-fours that were heavier than you are to the top of four-story buildings."

"Up a ladder?"

"On a lift," Mark admitted with a husky laugh. "Madam, your bedroom."

"I thought we changed *my* bedroom to *our* bedroom last night."

"Remember? I told you I'd ask, give, but never take. I don't make many promises, but I try to keep the few I do make."

What about "until death do you part"? Sara silently questioned. She'd taken her marriage vows as the most sacred of promises. Mark hadn't. He'd done the honorable thing and married her to legitimize their unborn child. She should have realized that coercion and duress nullified his material promises.

She couldn't ask the question constantly nagging her. He'd been home less than forty-eight hours. Major miracles took longer to accomplish. By asking, she'd be flirting with an honest reply that she felt certain would break the fragile ties between them.

"I understand," Sara whispered, slipped her shirt over her head to hide her anxiety for the future. She thought she heard him murmur "I doubt it," but he'd stepped into the bathroom before she said, "What?"

"I'm going to shave," Mark replied, his heart sinking to his heels when she refused to be coaxed into saying what he desperately needed to hear.

They were right back where they started five years ago. Only this time she didn't bother to justify sharing his bed because she loved him. How many times had she promised to love him forever? By telling her how he kept the few promises he'd made, he'd expected her to vow eternal love.

He ran hot water over the bristles of his shaving brush, then swirled it against the soap in the mug. The long and the short of it could be boiled down to one simple fact, he realized: She didn't love him. He kept setting the conversations up to give her opportunities to tell him, but she didn't. He blew it when he walked out. He'd had the whole world in the palm of his hand and he couldn't keep it.

He lathered his face with deliberate viciousness.

She didn't love him.

His blue eyes closed. The razor in his hand slipped, nicking his jaw.

"Damn!"

"What?" Sara called.

"I cut myself." He was bleeding to death inside! "It's nothing."

Quietly Sara pulled open the bottom drawer of the dresser. The grand-finale purchase lay undisturbed on top of her other nightgowns. Beth Ann had insisted she buy it without trying it on first. She held it up by the skimpy shoulder straps. It didn't look this . . . She couldn't think of a word to describe the sheerness of the garment. What would Mark think if he saw her lounging on the bed in this poor excuse for a nightgown?

He'd think she bought it especially for his delight, she mused with a catlike grin on her face.

Sara heard Mark turn the water off in the sink.

Deciding to use all her ammunition to fight for her cause, she hastily donned the nightgown. Within seconds she was lying on the bed in what she hoped was a seductive pose.

"I'd better take a shower," Mark shouted, quietly adding to himself, "An ice-cold shower ought to clean up my lust." She didn't love him. Want him, perhaps. But he hadn't given her much choice with his bulldozer tactics.

"You took a shower after the tennis match. Do you think you need one?" Sara called. Fidgeting, drawing the filigreed lace of the plunging neckline a fraction of an inch higher, she glanced from the bathroom door to the mirror above the dresser, which was across from the bed.

Her mouth circled into a gasping "Oh!" Talk about letting it all hang out! There was hardly anything hanging *in!*

"Cooking over a hot stove . . ." The rest of

114

his explanation was drowned out by the noise of the shower.

Sitting up, Sara stared at herself in the mirror. The designer who whipped up this frothy piece of nothing certainly knew his business, she thought. Her fingers traced the lines of the black lace that accentuated the rosy fullness of her nipples. The same double threads formed a seductive swirling pattern below her waist, leaving her upper thighs and long legs, for all practical purposes, naked.

"You look like a soiled dove," she whispered aloud, choosing a polite version of the word used to describe woman's oldest profession.

Sara sprang from the bed. The idea was to be provocative, not obscene!

Peeling the confection over her head, she neatly folded it and returned it to the bottom drawer. The pendulum of choice swung to the other direction as she chose a prim, high-necked, long-sleeved gown.

Shivering, Mark lathered himself, paying particular attention to thoroughly soaping his hands. What he needed to do was show her that sex wasn't the reason he wanted to share her bed.

He directed the nozzle of the shower to a lower position. The impact made his teeth chatter.

She probably thought she meant less to him than a quick roll in the hay. But how could he convince her otherwise? By keeping his hands to himself, he thought wryly, and not resembling a rock every time he got within ten feet of her. Mark groaned. Dammit, involuntary reflexes couldn't be controlled. There were boundaries to his restraint.

He sloshed frigid water across his face, then shut the water off and glanced at himself. Respectably unobtrusive, he noted with grim satisfaction. The difficult part ahead would be to keep his mind on sleeping rather than doing what came naturally when a man went to bed with his attractive wife.

Hadn't he read somewhere that sex was a mental, as well as a physical, exercise? Tonight he'd discover the truth. He'd occupy his thoughts with using his hands constructively, building a dream house in his mind.

After drying himself he took his robe from the hook on the back of the door, shoved his arms into sleeves, and drew it together at the waist with a double knot of the sash.

The first order on the agenda for Monday, he told himself, would be to buy a pair of flannel pajamas. Clenching his teeth together to keep them from chattering, he realized that the drastic change in body temperature made him a prime candidate for pneumonia.

Sara's eyes rounded as she watched Mark flip back the covers and reach over to turn the light off. "You're sleeping in your robe?"

"I must be coming down with a cold or something." Mark rolled toward the wall and mentally began sketching a blueprint of that dream house.

Reaching across his shoulder, Sara touched the side of his face. "You're freezing!"

"Yeah. There's a flu bug going around. Some of the carpenters have been sick."

"You felt fine earlier, didn't you?"

"Uh-huh." He pictured the bold line indicating the thickness of the concrete foundation. "Charlie, the building superintendent, said it hit him like a sledgehammer."

"That's probably why you were breathing hard when you carried me upstairs."

"I'll be all right. A good night's sleep and I'll be as fit as a fiddle tomorrow."

Sara lay her head back on her pillow, stifling her disappointment. "Are you running a temperature?"

With several quick mental strokes Mark added the interior walls to the house, careful to indicate which way the doors would open and close. Her hand, which remained on his shoulder, threatened to destroy his powers of concentration. He lightly patted her hand, then shrugged his shoulder to remove it.

"Hot and cold flashes," he mumbled through clenched teeth.

Sara remembered how Mark didn't like to be babied when he didn't feel well. It was as though he didn't want her to be anywhere around him when he was weak. She curled the hand he'd shrugged off under her pillow.

"Can I get you anything? Aspirin?"

"Go to sleep, Sara. I'll be fine."

"Don't I get a good-night kiss?" she asked prettily, reluctant to go to sleep without a small measure of affection.

117

Tempted to roll over and taste the sweetness of her lips all night, Mark skillfully imagined indicating on the blueprint the steps leading to the second story. "Better not. I wouldn't want you to get my germs."

"Don't be ridiculous. We swapped germs downstairs," Sara replied with a snap of frustration.

"I wasn't feeling bad then. Good night, honey." Pleased with himself for making his mind devoid of lustful thoughts, he made a mistake by letting his hand reach back to stroke the gentle curve of her hip. The blueprint disintegrated, replaced with a lush picture of Sara's figure. He groaned aloud, jerking his hand to his side, and ground his teeth together in concentration.

Hearing the groan, Sara wrapped her arm around his waist. "Mark! Are you in pain?"

Above all else he had to get Sara back on her side of the bed. "Hot flash. Please, Sara, let me go to sleep."

Feeling rebuffed but knowing how he was when he was sick, Sara moved to the edge of the mattress on her side. "Good night."

For what seemed like hours she stared into the darkness at Mark's rigid back. She waited to hear his breathing slow to an even pace, but the sound she heard frightened her. It alternated from shallow pants to deep breaths, which made her wonder how his lungs could accommodate such huge drafts of air.

Mark focused his thoughts on the physical exertion of fastening the partition lumber to the concrete foundation. As he pictured himself single-handedly carrying the hundreds of pounds of weight, a thin sheen of perspiration beaded on his upper lip. Build a house for Sara, he silently chanted as he pounded nails into place.

Long after the sun rose, Mark placed the last row of shingles in place. The house was finished, and so was he. Exhausted, he fell into a deep sleep.

Sara glanced at the clock on the night table. Six o'clock Monday morning, she thought, wondering if she should awaken Mark. In less than a half hour his foreman would be calling the house to make certain that their orders hadn't been changed over the weekend.

"Mark?" she whispered, lightly shaking his shoulder.

There was no response.

He must still be sick, she deduced, knowing that the slightest noise usually awakened him. She eased herself from beneath the covers, then rose carefully. Certain that the phone on his side of the bed would begin ringing within minutes, she tiptoed around the bed and unplugged it.

Her face level with his, she noted the thin lines of fatigue sketching his brow. Obviously, she decided, he was too sick to go to work. Instinctively she wanted to brush back the damp lock of hair from his forehead to test his temperature. Torn between waking him to get him to take some medicine and letting him sleep, she decided that sleep was the best cure.

As silently as possible she gathered the clothes

119

she needed to get dressed for work, then moved through the door, into the hallway.

She ran lightly down the steps, certain that the shrill ring of the phone was only moments away. Should she answer it, she wondered, and make business decisions for Mark? Shaking her head, she decided to tell his foreman that Mark was sick and wouldn't be in for the day. Before she left, she'd unplug the downstairs phone to insure no one would awaken him once she'd left the house.

The ring of the first call barely sounded when Sara grabbed the receiver.

"Manchester residence."

"Can I speak to Mark?" a brisk male voice inquired.

"He's sick. Can I take a message?"

"Sick? Is this the *Mark* Manchester residence? I must have the wrong number."

"Mark is sick."

Sara listened to the stranger chuckle. "He'd have my job for—"

"Look, whoever you are . . ." Sara began to rant in defense of Mark's workaholic reputation.

"Charlie, ma'am. I didn't mean to imply—"

"Then don't! Now, do you need equipment or supplies that haven't been delivered to your job site?" she questioned, taking a pad and pencil from a drawer. Those were similar questions to ones she'd heard Mark ask on other mornings during breakfast.

"Ma'am, I'm just calling like Mark told me to do. Did he mention whether or not he wants me to drop a check off at the supply company?"

Sara bit her lip. Making quick decisions concerning something about which she hadn't the least idea wasn't her forte—especially before several cups of coffee.

"He must want you to pay them if he gave you a check," she said, thinking aloud.

"Maybe you'd better ask Mark."

In her best schoolteacher voice Sara replied, "That won't be necessary. Pay them."

"But—"

"And be certain to get lien wavers," she added, remembering Mark's instructions to another foreman from months back.

"Well, if you say so, ma'am. I'd feel a lot better if I could talk to Mark, though."

"That isn't necessary. If you have any problems, have the supplier call here immediately," she bluffed.

"Tell Mark I hope he feels better," Charlie tacked on with uncertainty. "Sure hope this check doesn't bounce like the last one did. Bye."

Sara stared at the receiver as though it had turned into a reptile. Bounced check? She tapped the button to restore the connection with Charlie. Why hadn't Mark said something about the overdrawn account to begin with?

She couldn't believe that Mark was in such poor financial shape that he'd write a bad check, but evidently this wasn't the first one. Mark must have told Charlie to hold the check and he'd try to stall payment until the merger went through.

Afraid that she'd really messed up, she reached

down and unplugged the phone before another call would demand other decisions.

Any fading doubts she had regarding the necessity for Mark's return to the homefront grew stronger. He had to return to assure the deal going through. Obviously he was in dire financial straits.

She put the coffee on and changed clothing as she rehashed the conversation to make sure that she understood what Charlie had said. It didn't take a financial wizard to know that a building contractor who gave a supplier a bad check wasn't going to be in business very long. The first thing the supplier would do would be to refuse to send materials needed to complete a job. No materials being delivered would delay completion schedules, which would delay draws for money. A vicious cycle spun in dizzy circles through her mind.

How much money did Mark need? she wondered. Teachers were notoriously underpaid, but she'd deposited the vast majority of the money Mark had given her during their separation. Would that, plus the amount she had in her savings account, be enough to get him out of the red?

She poured herself a cup of coffee, thoughtfully sipping the brew.

Any amount had to help, she decided. But how was Mark going to react to taking money from her? He'd insisted that she spend her salary on frivolous things she wanted for Jamie, herself, or the house. On the one occasion, early in their marriage, when she'd suggested that they budget their income and each pay their share of the bills, Mark had calmly informed her that he was perfectly capable of supporting her and their unborn child.

His pride wouldn't allow financial aid from his wife.

To hell with his male ego, she thought, fuming, then went to the desk drawer and pulled out the savings account passbook. The drive-up windows would be open at the bank before school started. She'd leave ten dollars in the account to keep it active and deposit the remainder in Mark's business account. Regardless of how much or how little he owed, a few thousand dollars could make a difference.

After she shrugged her shoulders into the muted pink-and-gray plaid jacket that matched her linen skirt, she straightened her shoulders as though preparing for battle. Picking up her purse, she made certain that the cosmetics she needed were in the bottom, then she strode out the front door. She could dither later. The drive-up window at the bank opened at seven. She'd be there, first in line.

Mark needed her help and she was going to give it . . . whether he wanted it or not.

CHAPTER EIGHT

For three weeks Sara lived on raw nervous energy. Mark turned her world upside down with his unpredictability. She expected him to immediately discover the additional money in his business account and blow his cork. But if he did realize that she'd given him her money, he didn't say anything.

Sara also expected him to make physical advances. Each night he politely kissed her forehead, rolled over, and snored. Snored, for heaven's sake! Until his brief illness, he'd never snored.

Then, too, she expected him to badger her about attending the Moran barbecue. He didn't mention it.

And where were the gifts he'd showered on her throughout their marriage? Her suspicions as to his ailing bank balance were confirmed by his coming home empty-handed. Sara comforted herself with the thought that at least she didn't have to feel guilty about him spending money he didn't have in order to buy her trinkets.

While exchanging confidences with Beth Ann, Sara temporarily felt reassured that everything would work out for the best. At Beth Ann's persistence Sara had given in to her friend's capricious whim for her to wear the black, lacy nightgown. Feeling silly as all hell, she'd carefully scrutinized Mark for his reaction. Now, as she pushed her cafeteria macaroni and cheese around on her plate, her cheeks burned with humiliation at his complete lack of interest. Oh, yes, he'd swallowed hard, but Sara didn't know whether he was swallowing back his embarrassment at finding her in such a ridiculous outfit or whether he was attempting to keep from throwing up. She hadn't had the courage to ask.

There were other peculiar things he did, too, she mused. What method of madness was behind the annoying habit he'd acquired of opening her top dresser drawer and staring into it when he thought she wasn't there? That, combined with his other unprecedented activities, bothered her. She hadn't put anything unusual in there. Unable to figure it out, she'd removed everything in a frenzy of paranoia. Gloves, handkerchiefs, and scarves revealed no clue to his unusual behavior.

The other thing Mark had done over the past few weeks was to talk about Jamie. At the dinner table he'd recall humorous anecdotes. Lingering guilt over Jamie having been in her care at the time of the accident made her anticipate some sort of recriminations. Again Mark did the unforeseeable. Not once did he accuse of her neglect, nor did he suggest starting another family, as he had on the day of his return. In fact, he had suggested permanently taking care of the birth-control problem.

Sara had been speechless. In his unflappable way he'd simply said that a vasectomy was something for him to think about. He didn't want her to worry about another unexpected pregnancy.

A curl of macaroni slithered off the edge of the plate.

One of them was losing their mind! Certain that she was the one who needed to make reservations at the funny farm, she outwardly gave the usual calm, serene appearance to the casual observer, but inside she was a total wreck.

"He must have forgotten that it takes two to make babies," she muttered as another piece of macaroni eluded the tines of her fork.

"Stab it," Jared suggested, seating himself across from her.

"And have you accuse me of passive aggression? I know how your convoluted logic works."

"Ouch! Open hostility? For lunch?"

With a swift apology Sara acknowledged the unjustified remark. Since he'd played tennis with Mark, at least the questions Jared asked seldom required self-analysis.

"Jeff Larkins. Did he make it to your office?"

she asked when the silence between them became awkward.

"I just left him with a pack of crayons and a sheet of blank paper."

"As angry as he was when he stormed from my class, you'll probably find confetti and wax spots on your carpet when you return."

Mark's trained eyes carefully observed her tense posture. His theory that laughter cured most problems suffered with her caustic remark, a weak attempt at humor.

"Jeff suppresses his emotions at home and acts in a bizarre manner at school. He's drawing a family portrait . . . as he sees it. If I asked you to draw a picture of Mark and yourself, what would I see?"

Sara realized that Jared had held his inquisitiveness in check but had decided to revert to his usual psychological tactics. She appreciated his concern. And yet, she'd made a pact with herself that she'd resolve her problems with Mark on her own.

"Oh, I don't know," she answered, copying Beth Ann's rambling style of speech. "Mark is taller, broader than I am. Angular. Sharp corners. Maybe I'd do him in squares and rectangles. But then again, I could make him one solid triangle. You know, base of the triangle representing his broad shoulders . . . the narrowing point representing—oh! He wouldn't have any legs then, would he? Hmmm, guess I'd put two upside-down bowling pins under the triangle. As for myself—shorter, rounder. A circle. Perhaps a series of circles in all the right places. On second thought, since this is supposed to reveal psychological undertones"—she cast him a devilish glance as she paused for a breath—"I guess a woman who champions equal rights should draw both the bride and the groom the same height. Of course, I'd have to make my heart as big as his head—"

Jared raised his hands to stop the patter. "Okay, okay! This reminds me of the classic case that nearly destroyed the hypothesis of my doctoral dissertation. Using a class of first-graders as a control group, I had them do a series of pictures. Each day I'd arrive, bright and cheerful, expecting to find behavior patterns through their drawings. I'd pass out the stack of paper and a huge box of crayons for them to splatter their most secret feelings on." He paused when he observed Sara straighten attentively. "Billy Patterson. I'll never forget that kid's name if I live to be a hundred."

"What did Billy Patterson draw?" Sara asked when she thought Jared was going to drift away from the subject.

"Billy drew his family, his house, his favorite toy, *everything*, in browns, purples, blacks, and grays," Jared answered in a hushed tone. "Classic manic-depressive pictures. A real Charles Manson in the primary grades. I loved it. At night I'd dream about saving this child from himself."

"Well?"

"Well, what?" Jared said teasingly as he forked some peas into his mouth.

"What became of the satanic Billy Patterson?"

"The last I heard, he'd graduated from college with a sociology degree and had volunteered for a Peace Corps program."

Sara instinctively knew that she was being suckered in but couldn't keep from saying, "So much for crayons and paper!"

"Oh, I still believe that under the right circumstances they're a useful tool. I just have to be careful."

"All right. I'll bite. Why do you have to be careful?"

Jared grinned. "Because if the child sits in the back of the room and the kids in the front of the room pick the yellows, reds, greens, and blues, that only leaves—"

"The purples, grays, browns, and blacks," Sara completed with a groan.

"There's a moral to the story that applies to you."

"Dare I ask what on a full stomach?"

"You don't have to, but I'm hoping you will."

"As the kids say, 'Lay it on me.' "

"Given a choice, Billy would have chosen the bright side of life. I think, given the same choice, you would too. Maybe it's time for you to step to the front of the room. Get your hands on some bright colors. Oh, it isn't as safe. The teacher is within striking distance. She'll see each and every mistake you make, but—"

Sara cocked one eyebrow. "Haven't you forgotten something? I'm the teacher, the lady behind the desk."

"Here, yes, but not at home." Extending his own theory, Jared asked solemnly, "Do you know what happens when you mix blue, yellow, green, and red? All those radiant, cheerful colors denoting happiness? You get brown, gray, and purple."

"Meaning that I need to separate each problem and stick to one color?"

"It's worth thinking about. Maybe your anger about Jamie's death is entangled with your love for Mark. The frustration you feel about people who drink and drive is mixed with your benevolence toward Beth Ann. Could it be that you've tried an emotional jump from blacks and grays, expecting to get pure yellows and reds?"

Contemplating his theory, Sara moved her knife and fork to the center of her plate. Before she could reply, she heard Jared's name being called on the loud speaker system.

"Uh-oh. I told the office to call me if Jeff started drawing obscene pictures on my walls. Would you mind taking my tray back?"

"Sure."

Sara watched Jared's lanky form rushing toward the double doors. She hadn't eaten much, but Jared had given her plenty of food for thought.

Mark sliced the carrots, celery, onions, and ginger root as he hummed along with the music on the radio. Beside Sara's place setting on the table, he'd stacked the signed petitions that he'd procured for MADD. An original David Lee watercolor lay hidden beneath the pile of papers.

The purr of her sporty convertible pulling in the driveway brought a wide grin to his face. She'd risen holy hell when he'd given her the car for their third anniversary. But he'd turned a deaf ear to her protests. It pleased him to buy things for her that she wouldn't buy for herself. That, coupled with his strong aversion to working on automobile engines, which invariably stained his hands with oily grime, was plenty of reason for the gift.

He rinsed his hands and wiped them on the dishcloth.

Sara schooled her facial features from a wary scowl into what she hoped would pass as a polite smile. She wondered how he could quit in the middle of the afternoon, before his crews had reported in to the office. For a person who should be worried about keeping the creditors away from his door, he appeared totally relaxed. Months ago, before he'd walked out on her, he'd worked horrendously long hours. Fatigue had etched tired lines on his face. Obviously money wasn't the problem then. He'd preferred to stay at the office to avoid coming home to her. The smile slipped into a grimace.

Was she mixing her colors again? she silently questioned, realizing that she'd blended financial problems with personal problems. One color at a time, she instructed herself.

"You're home early," she said as she deposited her grade book and papers on the kitchen counter.

Mark spread his arms, gesturing between the

131

table and the carefully prepared ingredients on the counter. Hungrily his blue eyes, in an all-inclusive sweep, followed the line of her bent shoulders to the delectable curve of her narrow waist.

"I thought I'd surprise you. Wives are supposed to go wild for husbands who fix dinner and bring presents."

Another surprise, Sara thought. His unpredictable behavior had her mind spinning dizzily. Oh, what she'd give for a sane, humdrum life other women complained about!

"Nice," she commented noncommittally.

"Not exactly a response to be classified as 'wild,'" Mark muttered. He turned back to the sink, hiding the tremor of his hands under a stream of cold water. "Your gift is beside your plate."

Sara realized that she'd disappointed him with her lack of enthusiasm, but the thought of his starting the gift routine again made her angry. "You shouldn't waste your money on me."

"I don't consider it a waste."

"Money isn't everything. It won't buy happiness," she said, instantly regretting having voiced trite clichés, when she turned and saw the stack of papers on the table. She immediately recognized the printed forms, now with two columns of signatures. Her eyes flooded unexpectedly as she glanced from Mark's gift to the man rigidly standing at the sink scrubbing his hands meticulously.

Twisting at the waist when he heard her sob, he

132

saw her cover her face. "Sweetheart? Oh, sweetheart, I didn't mean to make you cry. . . ."

Feeling herself being enfolded in his strong arms, Sara gave way to the wall of tears she'd blocked since Jamie's death. His unexpected kindness unhinged her. No accusations, no recriminations, only hours spent accumulating signatures when he should have been working. The red haze she'd seen when she'd thought he'd spent money on her, washed by the transparency of her tears and the warmth coming from his broad chest, changed to a rosy-pink glow.

"I'm sorry," she said, panting between uncontrollable bouts of tears. "It's silly. I don't know why I'm soaking your shirt."

"Go ahead. Cry it out. You'll feel better," he whispered, holding her close, soothing her with his callused hands.

Unsuccessfully wiping at her eyes to stem the tide of tears, she didn't resist when Mark cradled her head against the warm curve of his neck and shoulder. "I miss Jamie. I loved him so much. Why? Why him?"

"I've asked the same questions a million times," Mark replied huskily. His hands gently kneaded the tight muscles along her spine. "Better me than him."

"Or me. Why not me? I was there." As she felt a sharp bolt of tension stiffen Mark's body, she wrapped her arms around his shoulders. "I didn't mean—"

Mark shuddered. "I've cursed myself for not being there."

"No." The thought of Mark being with Jamie, of him trying to stop the force of the wayward car with his own body, brought a resurgence of tears. "You couldn't have stopped the car."

"You couldn't have, either. Can you ever forget what I said at the hospital? I was crazy. The message I received was garbled. I didn't know what had happened. I pictured you and Jamie . . ." His hands tightened convulsively around her waist. Her slight gasp made him realize that his hold threatened to break her fragile ribs. "Guilt made me say those inexcusable things. If only—"

Sara reached up and silenced his incriminations with her fingers. Blinking to clear her vision, she shook her head. "Don't. I'm to blame."

"You?" His hand cradled the side of her face, and he captured the tear threatening to splash from her dark eyelashes with his thumb. "Never."

He searched her eyes for any hidden recriminations. He couldn't believe that she'd blamed herself for the accident. Vulnerable, he thought, amazed that her feelings of guilt matched his own. Didn't she realize that it was his unworthiness that had caused the problems? His inability to hold his company together that had made him skulk away from his family? She didn't. He'd recognize disdain. Lord knew he'd seen enough of it in his youth.

Mark brought her forehead to his lips, and his heart swelled with love. Never again, he silently vowed, never again would he let his incompetency in business endanger their marriage. Never.

A long sigh escaped Sara. He didn't blame her. Swallowing, she tasted the saltiness of her tears. She felt as though the weight of the world had shifted from her shoulders.

Mark restrained from letting his lips close over hers. He wanted to assuage her grief with tender, healing loving. His chest expanded to accommodate the burst of emotions within. A familiar surge of hot blood coursed through him.

She'd given him a rare gift: forgiveness. As much as he wanted her, he couldn't defile her generosity by making physical demands.

Sara felt his chest extend beneath the heel of her hand. His heart thudded irregularly for a few seconds, then returned to its normal pace. Loosening her curled fingers, she saw the damp, wadded fabric of his shirt.

"I've made a mess of your shirt," she said inanely, acutely aware of a deep yearning she couldn't express without seeming insensitive. "Next time I'll use a handkerchief," she promised with a watery smile. "Can I help with the rest of dinner?"

"Set the wok on the burner and let it start heating," he replied absently, thinking of another handkerchief, another stain, another wound being healed by caring hands.

"Mark?" As she softly called his name she imagined a rosy-pink rainbow arching between them. "Thanks for getting the petitions signed."

"You're welcome." Mark opened the refrigerator to get a pound of butter. "They were only part of the gift. Look on the bottom of the stack."

Sara set the wok in its stainless-steel holder, which snuggled over the burner. On the tip of her tongue hung the protest: You shouldn't have. Knowing that it was useless, she slowly crossed to the table and removed the petitions to reveal a small, framed watercolor.

"It's beautiful," she said, admiring the work of her favorite artist. White flowers tinged with pink centers, painted in a formal Japanese arrangement representing sun, moon, and earth, were nestled on a teal-blue background.

"It's an original, not a copy." Mark studied the fleeting mixture of emotions crossing her face. Admiration, a flash of joy, quickly followed by a frown of dismay.

"We can't afford an original David Lee."

Mark chuckled. "Polite etiquette says you're to graciously accept the gift with a charming thank-you. Don't worry. We can afford it. Right after I sign the merger papers I'll be able to buy a dozen paintings. Business will triple in size."

Sara put the painting down, as though it were as hot as the wok. Would the check he'd issued to pay for it bounce from one end of Missouri to the other? Her teeth bit the fleshy lining of her lower lip. Was this a bribe to make her accompany him to the Moran's country house? Or was it a good-bye gift?

Unable to express her deepest fear—his permanent departure—she asked, "Can you afford this before the merger?"

"I'm not exactly broke right now," he stated firmly.

"Not exactly?"

Mark dumped the fresh vegetables into the wok and stirred them with vigor. Any financial disclosure threatened him. He regretted the necessity to continue pretending that he'd come from the same type of middle-class background as Sara, but he'd lived the lie too long to let a few soul-sharing minutes weaken the protective wall that hid the truth. She'd pity him. Pity was a poor substitute for the love he craved.

His silence forbade further questioning.

"I appreciate the thought behind the gift," Sara asserted softly, "but I know your business needs the capital more than I need a David Lee original hanging on the wall."

The metal utensil he used to stir the vegetables clanged against the metal rim as he wheeled around. Had she slapped him, the effect of her intentions would have been the same. "You will *not* return the painting."

"I'll deposit the money in the company account."

"The hell you will."

Sara shivered beneath the tone of his voice and his icy glare. Having gone too far to retreat, she defiantly raised her chin. "I've already deposited my savings into your account."

"You *what?*"

"I said—"

"I heard what you said. I want an explanation. Pronto!"

Sara smelled the vegetables burning, saw the

black smoke billowing from behind his back. "Dinner's burning."

"Then we have something in common. So am I!"

He reached around and turned the burner to the "off" position, then stalked toward her. Step by step she retreated, until she felt her back touch the wall. Mark extended both of his arms forward, blocking any further retreat. "What made you have the audacity to deposit money into my account?"

"You had a check bounce," she answered, her mouth dry. She couldn't tell him who told her without involving Charlie. There wasn't a doubt in her mind that Charlie would be standing in the unemployment line if she revealed her source.

"Never," he vowed. "I don't write bad checks. In case you aren't aware of it, there are laws against writing hot checks. Who spread that filthy lie?"

Instinctively Sara placed her hands against his chest to prevent him from coming closer. "I can't tell you."

"Why? Don't I have the right to face the person?"

Sara tried to think of a way to verify her information without incriminating Charlie, but with Mark so close, her mind malfunctioned. "It's a reliable source."

Muttering an expletive she'd never heard him use, he dropped his arms and shook his head. A number of times when he'd been a kid he'd been accused of minor crimes. The accuser was always unidentifiable, but the accuser's word was always above reproach. It sickened him.

Somewhat shocked, Sara shifted from one foot to the other. She sensed that she'd offended more than his sensibilities. He looked physically ill.

"I'll have the bookkeeper send you a copy of the company bank statement." Mark pivoted toward the back door and left without another word.

Uncertain of how she could have misinterpreted what Charlie had said, Sara nevertheless knew that she'd made a dreadful mistake.

"Mark!" she yelled.

The door slammed before she could stop him from leaving. She ran across the kitchen, opening the door. Mark stood beside the house staring up at the sky, his hands knotted deep in his pockets.

"I must have made a mistake," she apologized. "Forgive me?"

CHAPTER NINE

Mark wasn't certain he'd heard Sara call to him or whether his subconscious had bellowed, Don't go!

Why stay? She didn't love him. Dammit, she believed he was destitute.

He stood rooted to the ground, unable to get to his car, unable to return to the house, unable to do anything other than raise his face to the late-afternoon sun. Eyes closed, he heard the distant traffic, smelled the scent of the Missouri River.

His stomach wrenched with the idea that sooner or later he'd have to tell Sara how the thought of being poor again made him break out in a cold sweat. But not now, he temporized. Not now.

When?

The truth was, he couldn't tell her. How could he expect Sara to understand why he'd run like a scared dog months before Jamie's death when he couldn't verbalize the hellish nightmare of his past? He could almost feel the winter wind whistling through the boards of the two-room apartment his family had called home. Rancid smells teased his nostrils. All the soap in Dallas couldn't have kept him clean.

Heart sinking, he knew that protesting his pre-destined fate wouldn't change it. Welfare rolls increased, never diminished. Slum kids grew up to be unemployed bums. Pulling oneself up by one's bootstraps was the impossible dream.

"Forgive me?"

Through the blare of imagined horns he heard Sara's quiet plea. Forgive her? She represented everything good. Without her he was less than nothing.

The light essence of her perfume replaced the foul smell clogging his mind. Her soft hand warmly touching his arm restored heat to deep, immobilizing cold. A shadow of agony momentarily haunted the depths of his eyes as he opened them.

"Forgive me?" Sara repeated, uncertain that Mark had heard her.

His flesh was clammy beneath her hand. Small beads of perspiration dotted his upper lip. Sara frowned, concerned about the mysteriously reoccurring illness that kept his back turned toward her in bed.

"There's nothing I can forgive you for," he

answered softly, knowing that the blame for their problems rested on him. The dark, ugly secret had to be contained or he'd permanently lose her.

"I must have misunderstood. I'm sorry."

A crooked smile twisted Mark's lips. She misunderstood? He'd make certain that she couldn't understand. He'd die before revealing the truth. "It's okay, sweetheart. I'll deposit the money back in your account tomorrow."

Later that night as Mark lay huddled beneath a pile of blankets, curled toward the wall, Sara twisted the sheet covering her. The day had been difficult, but a curious feeling of satisfaction curved her lips. The muddy gray Jared had alluded to had two colors removed: pink and green. Green represented money. Pink represented guilt. One by one she promised to extract the colors that symbolized each problem that kept them on opposite sides of the bed.

With her cause—making Mark love her—clearly focused in her mind, she snuggled against his back.

Mark concentrated on regulating his breathing. The sensation of her breasts flattening against his back threatened his reins of control. Her stomach and legs intimately curving around his buttocks brought vivid images to mind. He listened closely for the simple words of love that would break the shackles.

Bleak silence.

His emotional thermometer hovered at the freezing point. Numb fingers drew the covers

142

tightly beneath his chin. With a silent curse he told himself that he was an optimistic fool to expect Sara to love him. His streetwise cunning and her blindness was what had enabled him to be with her in the beginning. Why couldn't he be content with sharing the house, the bed?

He had to stop thinking about rolling over and returning home. He'd hurt her enough. The bond of love they shared was gone. Jamie. Jamie. He missed his son. God, how he missed him.

With the familiar nightly litany distracting him from his physical longing for Sara, the frigid silence swallowed him as he drifted asleep.

Sara woke in a rush, disoriented. What day was it? Friday? Saturday? The phone rang incessantly. She glanced at the clock. The red digital numbers indicated ten minutes after five. Fumbling for the phone, she yawned.

"Hello?"

"Sara?"

"Beth Ann? Is something wrong?"

The weight of the bed shifted as Mark rolled to the center and sat up. Sara covered the receiver with her hand. "Go back to sleep. It's for me."

Sara heard a muffled sob from the other end of the line. "Beth Ann! What's wrong?"

"I need you! I'm at St. Joseph's Hospital."

"Where's Jared? Are you sick?"

"Jared left last night for a conference in Jefferson City. I'm not sick, but . . . could you drive over here? Please?"

"Sit tight. I'm on my way."

Sara sprang from the bed. "Something's wrong with Beth Ann. She wants me to meet her at the hospital." She quickly pulled a pair of jeans and a top from her dresser.

Mark pushed the covers back. "I'll go with you."

"No. You stay here. Call in sick for me, would you?"

"We'll call from the hospital." Mark went to the closet, shed his pajama bottoms, and yanked a shirt from the wire hanger. "Where's Jared?" he asked as he put on some jeans.

"Out-of-town conference. She said she wasn't sick. Why the hospital? That doesn't make any sense!"

He shoved his shirt into his slacks. "Maybe it's a relative."

"I'm ready." Sara searched her memory, but she couldn't recall Beth Ann mentioning having any relatives in the vicinity.

Minutes later they were in the car. In the dim light cast from the dashboard Sara watched Mark's jaw lock as he swiftly maneuvered the car out of the driveway. He'd taken charge the same way he had the morning she'd awakened with labor pains. Reflexively her hand brushed the front of her jeans.

"Stomach upset?" Mark asked with concern.

Sara shook her head, wondering how he'd seen the gesture in the darkness.

"I'll drop you off at the emergency door, then I'll park the car."

144

A flash of panic widened her eyes. The emergency room. That's where they'd taken Jamie.

"It's okay, sweetheart. I'll be there with you." This time, he added silently. He reached across with one arm and pulled her close to his side. Keeping his eyes on the street, he brushed his lips against her hair. He let down his defenses when she put her hand on his knee in a show of trust. "This time I'll be there if you need me."

Sara realized that the pain of losing a child wouldn't magically disappear with time. It would always be there. But with Mark standing beside her she could face it. Perhaps by sharing the hurt it would gradually lessen.

"Is that Beth Ann?" Sara asked, pointing toward the circular drive leading to the emergency door.

"Yeah. There's a parking place. Got a quarter?" Mark pulled into the empty space while Sara dug around in the bottom of her purse.

With a small, triumphant smile she held up a piece of change. Early in their marriage Mark had often teased her about buying a change purse, using coins instead of dollar bills. Once, when she'd playfully swung her purse at him, he'd accused her of attacking him with a deadly weapon. The weight of the coins was lethal, he'd gibed between shouts of laughter.

Mark took the quarter. As their fingertips met, he momentarily clasped hers, signifying that he remembered the same incident.

Funny, she thought, how in a time of stress the mind protects itself by thinking of better times.

145

She didn't wait for Mark to open her door. Faster than she was, he'd already twisted the lever on the parking meter when she strode to the front bumper.

"I'll be fine," she reassured him, noting his dark eyes quickly assessing her facial expression.

As they crossed the street he took her hand. Lifting it to his mouth, he caressed her palm with a whisper of a kiss. He had to help her anyway he could.

Beth Ann rushed to meet them, babbling, "Thank you for coming. I'm so scared. That could be me in there. I wasn't certain I should call. Maybe I shouldn't have. I can't think straight."

"Calm down, Beth Ann. First tell us what happened. Who's hurt?" Sara asked.

"Remember the friend I told you about?" she asked in a hushed voice.

Sara flattened herself against Mark's side. "No, Beth Ann. I can't."

"Please, Sara. His kidneys are malfunctioning. He—"

Visibly shrinking against Mark, Sara shook her head with vehemence. "Don't ask this of me. You're my friend. . . ."

"It's the man Jared told me about, isn't it?" Mark asked Beth Ann. He protectively pulled Sara closer as he felt her knees sag.

"He needs a chance. . . ."

Beth Ann rattled on incoherently, but Mark only heard the first words. Mark knew about desperately needing a chance, a good break in luck, an opportunity to do better. And he knew about guilt. Remorse. Self-condemnation. Compassion flooded through him.

"I'll see him. You take Sara back to the car."

"No!" Sara gasped, horrified. Her mind jumped back to seeing him barge through the doors of the emergency room. *Where's my wife, my son?* he'd shouted. *Where's the son of a bitch who hurt them? I'll kill him with my bare hands!*

She couldn't let Mark go in there.

Sara shrugged away from Beth Ann's hands, clinging to Mark's arm. If he avenged his son's death, she'd lose him forever. "Please, stay with me."

Mark felt compassion warring with his love for Sara. He wove his fingers into her hair, holding her head close to his heart. "Shh, sweetheart. Don't cry. This is something I have to do for both of us. We can't bring Jamie back to life, but perhaps we can make this man's death easier."

Totally befuddled by the unexpected twist, Sara straightened. She searched his face, looking for concealed anger. His dark eyes begged for understanding. Bitterness and hatred were transcended by the light of compassion beaming toward her. Sara gained strength from it.

"I'll go with you," she said.

"You don't have to," Mark said, realizing how difficult facing this man would be for her. "One of us is enough."

"No. We'll do it together."

* * *

An hour later Beth Ann thanked them tearfully, then waved as Mark pulled the car from the curb.

Staring through unseeing eyes Sara asked, "Do you think he'll live?"

"When I stepped out to call in sick for you, I talked to his wife. She doesn't have much hope."

"I felt sorry for her, for both of them. That doesn't make sense, does it? For months I hated him. Now I hate what happened, but . . ." Her words dwindled. Birth, life, and death happened with capricious disregard for the people whose lives were touched.

"Life seldom makes sense. Sometimes we try to control what happens, but destiny picks us up by the seat of the pants and gives us a swift kick in another direction."

From the corner of his eye Mark watched Sara. A lock of blond hair swept forward, curling softly against her neck. He wanted to stop the car and capture the tendril between his fingers, then lift it and kiss the pale skin where the wisp of hair had lain. He wanted to hold her, to tell her how proud he'd been of her back at the hospital.

In the months that they'd been apart, she'd grown. Where she used to avoid facing problems, she now confronted them. Hesitantly, perhaps, but when it came right to the wire, she rose to the occasion. He loved both the child-woman he'd married and the woman she'd become.

A niggling hope entered his mind. Would she show him the same gentle compassion she'd shown the man in the hospital? Remembering what she'd just said, he stilled the daydream. He didn't want her to feel sorry for him. Love and pity weren't the same.

"What are you going to do today?" he asked, pulling into the drive.

"I could go into work, but the substitute wouldn't be too pleased about scrambling to get ready and then having the teacher cheat them out of a day's pay by arriving at the last minute." She shrugged her shoulders. "I guess I'm stuck being a lady of leisure, huh?"

He almost asked if she wanted to go with him, but remembering that his schedule included inspecting several job sites that were none too clean, he said, "You should go back to bed. It's still early."

Sara opened her door. *Come with me,* she silently invited, *hold me, touch me, let me make believe that you love me.* She lowered her eyes to the purse in the space between them to keep him from seeing the wistfulness in them. "Maybe I will."

For Mark the thought of watching Sara crawl back into bed sent a shaft of awareness surging through him. His thoughts fragmented. Sara in bed. With him. Wrapped around him. Making sounds of pleasure. Wanting him. Loving him.

Cool it, he chided himself. He hadn't earned the right to ask for more than being a congenial roommate.

"I have a meeting with Moran at nine," he said, burying his yearning behind his business schedule. He turned the motor off and opened his door. As he unfolded himself from the car's interior he tossed over his shoulder, "Why don't you go buy something special to wear to the barbecue tomorrow?"

"Something appropriately black," she muttered morbidly. "Appropriate for the death of private ownership."

Mark courteously opened her door. "Did you say something?"

Determined to make one last appeal, she asked, "Are you certain that this is what you want to do? You won't be your own boss once you merge with Moran."

"There will be other compensations." He held his hand out to assist her from the car.

"Such as?" Her hand clung to his, her thumb stroking the back of his hand.

"A monthly salary. Company benefits. A share of the profits." Security, security, security, he recited mentally. With security on one side of the scale and personal satisfaction on the other, he knew which weighed the most. Pride had cost him too much already.

"What happened to your dream of having Manchester Builders being synonymous with the finest homes built in the area? Of hearing people say, 'That's a Manchester home'?"

Mark stepped ahead of her to unlatch the door. He couldn't deny the dream, but the near fatality of his company had cost him dearly. A dream wasn't worth the risk.

"I'll still be building houses."

She preceded him onto the screened-in porch, then into the kitchen. "But it won't be the same, will it? Moran builds look-alike row houses. Your houses have been moderately priced, but they had your stamp of individualism on them."

"Thanks." Since they'd seldom exchanged views on each other's work, he couldn't remember her voicing any opinion on his projects. "I'll still have input into what's incorporated into the blueprints."

"But it won't be the same, will it?" Although Sara wanted to fight for his dream, she knew that she'd lose. Mark had made up his mind to merge with Hal Moran.

"No."

"Then don't do it. Don't let your company be swallowed. Don't compromise quality for quantity," she argued. She crossed to where he stood in front of the sink, his back to her. "Don't compromise your life's dream."

Mark slowly turned toward her. "One-on-one tutoring, according to you, is better than a classroom of twenty or thirty. And yet you're a classroom teacher," he replied, reversing the logic.

"That's different," she protested. Automatically her hands reached up to still his head from shaking back and forth. "It is."

"How?"

"You're building houses. I'm—"

"Building the future of those kids." He grinned, certain that he'd won without revealing his fear of financial setbacks robbing him of his future with her. "And speaking of building, I'd better get dressed for work."

Frustrated by her lack of persuasiveness, she

followed him from the kitchen, up the stairs, and into the bedroom. There was a flaw in his logic. There had to be. But for the moment she couldn't find one.

She flopped on the bed when he went into the adjoining bathroom. "Are the merger papers going to be signed tomorrow at his house?" She shouted so he could hear her over the water gushing into the sink.

Mark rubbed the overnight growth of dark whiskers on his chin. Why didn't she drop it? he wondered. Recalling the discussion they'd had the previous night, he wondered if he'd thoroughly convinced her that he wasn't having money problems. He lathered the soft-bristled shaving brush and whisked it over the stubble, then started to shave. "Monday I'm supposed to meet him at the attorney's office."

"Hal wants to give me a once-over, doesn't he?"

"He knows who you are."

"Only as a teacher, not as the wife of a future partner."

"You worried about what kind of impression you'll make?" He wiped the residue of lather from his face and patted some after-shave lotion on the tender skin.

"Don't expect me to fawn all over him," she warned, wishing that she had the guts to refuse to make an appearance.

Mark poked his head through the open doorway. "Brownnose. That's what the kids call it, isn't it?"

"Whatever. I could really screw up the deal, couldn't I?" she asked as another alternative dawned on her. Moran would reconsider merging companies if she arrived in an outrageous costume and punctuated every sentence with a curse word.

"Don't," Mark said, his voice commanding. "This is important to me. I want you to be what you are. Sweet. Warm. Intelligent."

"Sounds like a well-trained bird dog," she retorted, sniffing indignantly.

Mark chuckled, moving toward the bed, drawn toward the gentle rise and fall of her breasts, the crook of her bent leg. "Fishing for compliments?"

Rolling her head from side to side, she said, "I know there's more to this merger than you're telling me."

"Your mouth puckered into a pout is sexy as hell," he praised.

"Don't sidetrack me with flattery. What are you hiding?"

"Flattery? Hiding?" He hitched the towel more tightly around his waist. "You're awfully suspicious lately."

"That's because you aren't yourself lately."

His eyes narrowed. Did she know something she hadn't confronted him with yet? he wondered, his heart thudding with fear. Had he inadvertently slipped in some way that she'd picked up on? He wiped his hands against the towel on his hips, almost dislodging it.

"Who am I?"

"A stranger. You sure as hell aren't the man I married."

Careful to ease himself onto the corner of the bed rather than pounce on her and demand an explanation, he quietly asked, "What do you mean?"

Sara had the overwhelming feeling that they were playing cat and mouse, and she was the mouse. Say the wrong thing and watch the cat spring, she thought silently. Her first impulse was to shrug her shoulders in dismissal to avoid facing the consequences of a rash reply. On second thought, she sat up and looked him squarely in the eye.

"You've changed."

"How?"

"Well, you didn't use to argue with me," she replied through tight lips.

"You used to constantly ask, 'What are you thinking about?' Now you know. What else?"

Listing his changes became increasingly difficult as he leaned toward her. She could see his dark pupils expanding, as though he heard her complaints with his eyes as well as his ears.

"I've seen you hunting through my top dresser drawer as though you're looking for something. You never did that before." Sara knew she continued to skirt around the main issues—Jamie and their lack of physical intimacy—but his nearness had her mind spinning.

"Simple. I like to look at your lacy underthings. Go on, now that you've started."

"Jamie. When you first came back, you couldn't say his name. Now . . ." Her voice trailed away.

"We both loved Jamie. We both miss him. Should we act as though he never existed? Shouldn't we talk about him?"

Sara nodded. "I'm not criticizing. I'm telling you how you've changed. That change was for the better."

Rising, reassured that she hadn't discovered his secret, he smiled. He was safe. She hadn't the foggiest notion of how much he'd changed over the years. "Any changes for the worst?" he asked, maintaining a casual tone in his voice.

The bed, she wanted to blurt, but realizing how silly saying *bed* instead of *sex* would sound, she hunted for another polite term. How could she ask him why he didn't make love to her without losing all sense of pride? Or worse, sound like a sex-starved nymphomaniac! That would be worse than dressing up in the slinky gown and seducing him. Besides, she knew that asking about their lack of lovemaking would lead to questions she couldn't dare ask: Why didn't he love her? Why did he leave her? How long would he stay this time?

"None," she murmured, hating herself for being a coward.

Inside the walk-in closet, Mark heaved a sigh of relief. One step at a time, he thought, coaching himself. According to Sara he'd changed for the better. Maybe with time, with unquestionable financial security, she'd learn to love him. Maybe.

155

He couldn't take anything for granted until he felt certain of himself.

Dressed in khaki-colored work clothes, he walked back into the bedroom. "In that case, I'll be going to work."

Sara lifted her chin off her chest, letting her eyes memorize him feature for feature. The anguish of not knowing whether or not he'd return made the mental snapshot important. Her dark eyes lingered on his narrow hips and broad shoulders, then lingered on the Manchester Homes logo above his shirt pocket.

"I'll have to buy new shirts for you," she said inanely, knowing that she wasn't making any sense to Mark.

Instantly Mark's level gaze dropped to his shirtfront, eyes straining to find a stain or tear. "Something wrong with this one?"

"There will be Monday. I imagine I'll have to remove the logo. Moran probably has one of his own."

At least he'd be able to afford new shirts, Mark mused, remembering a time when owning two shirts was a luxury beyond his means. "Most of the time I'll be wearing white shirts and slacks. From blue collar to white collar by merely signing my name on a sheet of paper." His attempt at adding levity by making fun of his mode of dress fell flat.

"Trading your carpenter's hammer for a pencil sounds like a bad deal to me," Sara demurred.

"Want me to plug the coffee in on my way

through the kitchen?" he asked, refusing to rise to her baited remark.

Sara clamped her teeth together as the chill that shivered through her each time Mark left her threatened to make her teeth chatter. Drawing her knees to her chest for warmth, she said, "No, thanks. I think I'll take your suggestion and sleep for a while. Bye."

Mark watched her pull the blankets from his side of the bed over herself and frowned. The sad note in her voice alarmed him. "You'll be okay?"

Sara wasn't certain that she'd ever be okay, but with a grunt she said, "Yeah."

As she heard his footsteps treading down the steps she wondered if people who lived in limbo could be described as being okay. Eyes closing, she pictured the map her class would be going over with the substitute teacher. She added new towns. Heaven to the north. Hell to the south. And somewhere in between was limbo.

CHAPTER TEN

"Sara, I believe you've met Hal Moran at school, haven't you?" Mark asked, introducing his wife to his future partner.

"Your son was in my class last year," Sara said to refresh her host's memory. He was the kid who crawled around the floor imitating a rabid Lassie, remember? she was tempted to add. The one who brought the cymbals to the auditorium and crashed them together after the principal's wel-come-back-to-school speech.

Hal took Sara's slender hand between his beefy palms. She concentrated on not flinching as she watched his eyes beam his approval of her gaily flowered jumpsuit. Even Hal Moran couldn't find anything objectionable in the throat-to-ankle-to-wrist garment, she thought self-consciously. The swirls of pink and blue flowers weren't nearly as eye-riveting as Hal's pink, green, and purple plaid slacks. The bright green polo shirt stretched tautly over the slight paunch at his waist. Only his dark hair, styled in a short, military crew cut, betrayed his casual golfer's attire. She knew from previous dealings with his son that Hal was extremely straitlaced.

"It's a pleasure to meet you on a more . . . agreeable occasion, Sara. For a while last year I thought I was going to have to build a padded cell for my wife and I. Isn't that right, dear?"

A small, thin woman in an outfit that matched Hal's peeked from behind her husband's brawny back and nodded. "I'm Martha. Can I get you something cold to drink?"

Sara noted that her voice resembled the whine of a whipped dog. The antagonism she felt toward Hal Moran intensified. Intuitively she knew that Hal Moran had smashed his wife's dreams and that Mark's were next on his agenda.

She glanced up at Mark to see his reaction. Mark's lips were smiling, but his blue eyes held the same look of resignation she saw in Mrs. Moran's. "No, I'm fine, thanks," Sara answered politely.

"Mark?"

"I'll have a Coke." Mark gestured toward one corner of the courtyard where other guests quietly milled around the shallow end of the pool. "I'll get it."

"Nonsense, my boy. Martha, Mark wants a Coke."

Sara withdrew her hand from between her

host's fingers. "Your home is lovely," she said when an uncomfortable silence fell between them.

Hal pounded Mark on the back. "Won't be long until you can afford a place in the country. Of course, as busy as I am, I don't spend much time here. But the little woman does. Says the chirping of the crickets soothes her nerves. Can't imagine what she has to be nervous about. She has everything."

Sara could. There wasn't a doubt in her mind that living with a drill sergeant in the Marine Corps would be preferable. Martha Moran probably exhausted herself meeting her husband's fetch-and-carry demands.

"Women and kids are impossible for men to understand," Hal added.

Tempted to throw a body block that would knock Moran into the pool, Sara knew that she had to get away from him or totally disgrace Mark. "Would you excuse me? I need to find the ladies' room."

"Martha?" Hal raised his hand and snapped his fingers.

"Never mind." Sara sighed, catching a windswept tendril of her hair with one hand. "There isn't much point in combing my hair."

Martha edged around her husband and handed Mark a bottle of Coke.

"Where's his ice?" Hal demanded, casting his wife a disparaging look. "Have Linda get it. That's what you hired her for, isn't it?"

Sara watched Mark's skin go white, then turn

beet-red. Good for Martha, she thought to herself, dubbing the lack of ice as a form of passive resistance on Mrs. Moran's part. Their son resorted to open rebellion at school to embarrass Hal, but obviously his wife had a more subtle approach to evening the score.

"I prefer mine straight out of the bottle," Mark said in deference to watching Martha make another trip. "Mrs. Moran, I heard about your rose garden. Would you mind if Sara and I strolled through it?"

Hal gave Mark another hearty slap on the back. Ignoring who the question had been addressed to, he answered, "Right down that path, my boy. I had each bush imported from an estate in England. They didn't want to sell them, but I made them an offer they couldn't refuse."

Cringing, Sara hooked her hand through the crook of Mark's arm, knowing full well that it was too early in the spring for the roses to be in full bloom.

With one final slap on Mark's shoulders Hal motioned toward the side of the courtyard. "You kids have a good time, now."

"You can't do it," Sara muttered as they turned the corner of the flagstone path. "No wonder their kid is screwed up."

"Hal's a good builder," Mark replied absentmindedly.

His hands were sweating so badly, he couldn't trust himself to put one on Sara's elbow to guide her over the steps. A woman, dressed in a black uniform with a frilly white apron, had caught his

161

attention within minutes of their arrival. What the hell was Linda Turnball doing here? he wondered. Why wasn't she in Dallas where she belonged? Don't panic, he warned himself. Chances were that she didn't recognize him.

"Did you see the way he treated his wife?" She watched Mark shrug his shoulders indifferently. "Not to mention the patronizing way he talked to you. Frankly, one more 'my boy' and I'd have shoved him in the pool."

"That's just his way of trying to make his guests feel as though they're part of the Moran family," Mark said, glancing over his shoulder to see if they were being followed.

"It's insulting. After being your own man and running your own company, how can you consider letting Moran get you under his thumb?"

"I'll manage."

Sara realized that she was getting nowhere fast by making Mark defensive. She tried another tactic. "It's beautiful here, isn't it?"

"Terrific," Mark said, seeing nothing other than a mental picture of Linda Turnball having an intimate chat with Sara. He knew that Linda could destroy everything he'd worked toward.

"Martha lives here from what I gathered."

"Yeah. Hal lives in town with their boy."

"When you make enough money, we could live that way." She injected a note of wistfulness to her voice. "I could retire from teaching, move to the country."

"Mmm." Preoccupied with keeping Sara and Linda apart, Mark hoped that his noncommittal responses were appropriate. The way his stomach was twisting into knots, he considered pleading illness and making an early departure. No, he couldn't do that. One more faked illness and Sara would haul him to the doctor. Besides, he couldn't afford to antagonize Hal Moran and expect the merger papers to be signed, sealed, and delivered on Monday. What the hell was he going to do?

"It doesn't seem to bother you that we'd be living apart," Sara grumbled, glancing at Mark from the corner of her eyes.

"Uh-huh."

Sara frowned, wondering what he meant by his response. Here she'd been gently leading him to discover for himself that the life-style of the Morans wasn't what he really wanted, and he hadn't heard a word she'd said!

"Mark? Are you listening to me?"

"Of course, sweetheart. I've heard everything you said. Moran's place is charming."

The schoolmarm in Sara made her want to demand that he repeat what she'd said to prove he hadn't been listening. Could it be that he didn't care whether or not they had a weekend marriage? Her frown deepened. Mark wouldn't have to worry about walking out again. He'd only have to put up with her two days a week. The rest of the time he could stockpile money or whatever else he'd been doing during their separation.

"I'm not going to quit teaching," she said assertively. Teaching and caring for Jamie were the only things that kept her sanity when Mark had

163

departed. She wasn't going to be stuck out in the boonies without anything to do other than mark the hours between sunrise and sunset by twiddling her thumbs waiting for the weekend.

Mark realized that he'd missed something in their conversation. "Fine, sweetheart. I want you to be happy."

"That's what I want for you, Mark. Don't kid yourself into believing that Hal Moran won't try to walk all over you. Within a year he'll cut you down until you won't be able to reach the first rung of a stepladder without standing on your tiptoes."

"I can take care of myself." Mark hid his fear of discovery behind a mask of cockiness. He grabbed Sara and hauled her against his chest. "Come here, woman. I'll take care of you too."

His switch from thoughtful introspection to ardent lover caught Sara off-guard. Her lips parted in an astonished gasp. There was a certain desperate quality in his lips as they closed over hers that puzzled her. This was a far cry from the friendly pecks on the cheek she'd received each night over the past few weeks.

The pent-up frustration she'd felt exploded in the back of her head as he wound his fingers in her hair, adjusting their mouths for deeper penetration. His other hand moved from her waist to her hips, pulling her tightly into his embrace.

Starved for his passionate kisses, her hands clung to his shoulders. Her tongue darted between his lips to taste the muffled tone of the groan coming from deep in his chest. When he held her, kissed her until she quivered in his arms, she knew why she loved him. Conflicts and doubts vanished.

"Mark! Where are you, boy?"

They sprang apart at the sound of Hal Moran's strident voice.

Mark silently cursed Moran's inopportune interruption.

"Hear his fingers snapping?" Sara blurted snidely.

"I'm coming, Hal," Mark shouted over his shoulder.

Sara took two steps backward. "By all means, don't let anything between us detain you."

"Sara, be reasonable."

"Reasonable?" Sara had never felt more reasonable in her life. "What happens when we're at home, doing more than kissing, and Hal summons you? Are you going to jump out of bed?" She whistled as though calling a dog. "Here, Mark. Come on, *boy!*"

"Come on, Mark, my boy," deeper male tones tinged with impatience echoed from the direction of the house.

"I have to go." One palm held upward, he silently pleaded for her to join him.

Slapping her would have been kinder. Sara had heard him say that same loathsome phrase months ago. She spun toward the rose garden. "Go ahead. Do what you have to do."

Mark's empty hand dropped to his side, clenching and unclenching in frustration. "I'll be back in a few minutes," he said as he turned and followed the flagstones back to the courtyard. "Wait here for me."

He'll be back, Sara mouthed, savagely wiping the imprint of his kiss from her lips. And she was supposed to be here, *serenely* waiting for his victorious return!

The old habit of avoiding confrontation by running suddenly held great appeal. Dammit, she'd tried to reason with him, hadn't she? Why should she stick around and kowtow to Hal Moran? Couldn't Mark see the writing on the wall? Hal Moran was going to bulldoze Mark the same way he rolled over Martha and their son. When reasoning didn't work, there wasn't any point in waiting for the inevitable.

She'd given it her best. Bluntly pointing out the future problems hadn't worked. Subtlety hadn't, either. What else could she do?

Sara caught her lower lip between her teeth. What she really should do was tell Hal Moran exactly what she thought of him and his merger! Her dark eyes widened. Why not?

Because Mark would throttle her for destroying the merger plans.

So? Would that be worse than watching Mark devoured inch by inch?

After all, hadn't the reason for her attending the barbecue been for Hal to discover what kind of woman Mark was married to? Was she a namby-pamby who could be pushed around?

Hell, no! she thought, pivoting on her heel and marching toward the courtyard. Her heart pounded in her ears at the prospect of waging all-out open warfare on Hal Moran.

She skirted through small clusters of guests, intent on reaching Moran before her courage failed. Pasting a sickly smile on her lips as she saw Mark talking to the maid, who was placing a tray on the cloth-covered banquet table, she wondered exactly what Moran had wanted Mark to do. Help serve?

"Well, well, there's the gorgeous little missus we were talking about," Hal said in greeting as Sara approached.

The condescending title razored up Sara's back. The idea that he'd been discussing her with a total stranger who was eyeing her as though she were an appetizer left few doubts as to the nature of the conversation.

"I think we need to have a little chat, Mr. Moran."

Hal winked, then, with a smirking grin, said to the tall hulk of man he'd been conversing with, "You'll excuse me, won't you, Bud? Seems Sara, here, wants to see me *alone.*"

The underlying insinuation that she was encouraging an intimate interlude with Mark's soon-to-be partner galled Sara. For a man who professed to be a pillar of the community with a purer than new-driven snow life-style to meaningfully squeeze her elbow and attempt to let his hand graze the side of her breast had Sara's palm itching to slap his face in front of everyone.

She caught Mark's eye as they passed by the banquet table. He flashed her an approving smile and continued to converse with the attractive hired help. Whatever Hal had asked him to do, Mark appeared to be enjoying it.

Mark narrowed his eyes, watching Hal escort Sara into the house. For a moment Sara diverted his attention from the crisis situation building between himself and Linda Turnball. He hoped that his forced smile equaled the serene composure of his wife's.

"That goody-two-shoes your wife?" Linda inquired, her resentment apparent.

"Yes."

Linda eyed Mark from head to toe. "How'd a man like you catch on to someone like her?"

"That's none of your business."

"Don't get uppity with me, buster. That sweet thing you married wouldn't touch you with a barge pole if she'd known you back in Texas."

Ignoring the truth, he asked, "What do you want?"

Each second he stood there talking to Linda endangered his achievement of the goal that was almost within his reach: financial security.

Streetwise, he knew that Linda saw him as a free meal ticket. She'd been a lazy, good-for-nothing kid. She hadn't changed. No doubt she still remembered him threatening to knock her head off if she kept extorting money from the smaller girls in the grade school they'd both attended.

He fingered the bills between the money clip in his pocket. Opening himself up for blackmail left a thick, sour coating on his tongue.

Linda snickered. "What goes around, comes around. Bet you thought you'd never see the day when you had to pay me."

"How much?"

"I'm tired of serving rich bitches." The snicker turned into a gold-digging smile. "How much you got?"

Never enough, Mark surmised from the glint in her pale eyes.

"You aren't going to bleed me dry." Mark risked a shot in the dark. "What do you think the Morans would do if I told them you attempted to blackmail their guest?"

"Makes no difference. I'm temporary help. Tomorrow I'll be back on the streets of St. Louis."

Mark noticed the trace of fear in her voice. "I could hire you. Give you a chance to make something of yourself."

"People like us don't get chances for nothing," she said with a snort. "We lie, cheat, and steal to make it from day to day. You're rolling high now, but it don't last long. You're gonna be right back in the gutter with me."

Mark recoiled. The smell of the streets had never left his memory.

"You know it. I know it." Linda filched a piece of ham from between a finger sandwich and crammed it into her mouth. She squirreled the meat to the side of her mouth. "Seeing as how you're doing so good, I wouldn't mind a small loan for old times' sake."

"For old times' sake," Mark muttered, pulling

his money clip from his pocket and peeling off several bills. "Never again."

"Just stick it in the apron pocket." Linda smiled triumphantly. She didn't want his stinking job. She wanted the good life. And Mr. Clean back there was going to give it to her. Bent over the table, she swayed her hips seductively against his front when he came close enough to shove the money in her pocket. Taffeta rustled over cotton. She gloated triumphantly. "Be seeing you."

"I'll see you in hell first." Mark gritted, swallowing to keep from gagging.

"Six of one, half a dozen of another." She shrugged. "Hell. The gutter. Ain't you learned that they both have the same street address?"

Hal motioned toward the loveseat. "What can I do for you?"

The double entendre wasn't lost on Sara. "Nothing, Mr. Moran. You don't have anything I want, including a partnership for my husband."

Seating himself, he let his eyes slowly peruse the woman who'd primly walked to the French doors overlooking the courtyard. Confidently he steepled his fingers.

"Mark feel the same way?"

"No," she answered honestly. "For some misguided reason he thinks the merger is essential."

"Money, my dear. Cold hard cash. Great motivator."

"We don't need . . . motivating."

Laughing, Hal lowered one hand to reach into the back pocket of his slacks. "You're a real hellion underneath that schoolmarm exterior, aren't you?"

"Let's keep this discussion on a business level, shall we?"

"Why? Once Manchester Builders becomes part of Moran Enterprises, we're going to get *very* close." He flipped open the personalized checkbook he'd removed from his pocket. "In fact, I'd be willing to make a generous donation to MADD. Too bad about your son. I read somewhere that eight out of ten parents end up in the divorce courts within a year. It would be a real shame." He shook his head.

Sara blanched at his audacity. In one long breath he'd propositioned her, given condolences, offered to donate money, and congratulated her on her upcoming divorce.

"Mail the check. Don't mislead yourself into thinking I'm for sale. Mark *may* agree to a merger, but he's possessive about his personal belongings," Sara retorted scathingly, glancing to the window. "You may get his business, but—"

Her rebuke died on her lips as she glanced through the small panes of the French doors and watched Mark close in behind the woman he'd been talking to, reach around her, and touch her below the waist. The rhythmical swaying of the woman's hips left little to Sara's imagination.

"Don't be naive, Sara. What makes you think Mark doesn't approve of our future relationship? Wasn't he eager for me to meet you? Did he stop us when he saw us coming in here?"

The hand she'd clamped to her mouth ground

painfully against her front teeth. She couldn't believe her eyes or her ears. Mark wouldn't make an assignation at Moran's party while throwing her into the arms of another man, would he?

"Did Mark say—"

"No." Hal rolled to his feet and hiked up his pants. "He's a man's man. Men understand these little indiscretions."

"You hypocrite," Sara managed to gasp. "You slimy ba—"

"Now, now, Sara. Don't hurl profanities at me."

She whirled from the windowpane she'd been staring through. "You made a mistake, Mr. Moran," she said icily. "This 'little woman' is going to tell her husband exactly what you've said."

"And what would that be?" Hal asked, feigning innocence as he laced his fingers together. "Aren't you going to appear foolish when I tell him that you expressed opposition to the merger and then misinterpreted some innocent remarks I made?"

"There was *nothing* innocent in what you suggested," Sara stormed.

"What did I say? That I'm looking forward to the partnership? That you're a hothead? Sounds innocuous to me," he said chidingly.

As she listened to Moran glibly twist the meaning of his words, Sara became paler and paler. Who would Mark believe? She'd damned her own evidence by telling him how straight Moran was. Less than ten minutes ago she'd told Mark that she objected to the merger.

Her eyes fluttered closed. A picture of Mark and a redheaded woman instantly flashed behind her lids. Her heart could deny what Moran had implied, but she couldn't allow herself to be a totally gullible fool and ignore what she'd seen.

Unable to withstand the results of the confrontation, she did what came naturally: she fled.

Half an hour later Sara backed her car from the dead-end gravel road she'd mistakenly turned down. She should have paid attention to where they were going when Mark was driving, she mentally scolded herself. She was lost.

Humorless laughter bubbled through her lips. Lost in more ways than one, she ruefully acknowledged. Mark had led her up the primrose path, and she'd blithely followed him without looking at the road signs. Why hadn't she realized how dangerous the course she'd mapped out was when he made love to her once and then lost interest? How could she have been stupid enough to ignore him when he told her his reason for returning? Why didn't she hear what he meant when he told her that he was considering a vasectomy rather than risk getting trapped by another pregnancy? Those were flashing red lights for any stupid fool, unless they were color-blind. In this case, blinded by love. A mirthless smile twisted her face.

She shifted the car into drive, wondering which way to turn. The winding country roads had her sense of direction thoroughly confused. She could go back the way she'd come, or she could keep traveling the other way.

"Keep going straight ahead," she decided, turning the steering wheel to the left. "Watch for signs . . . and don't cry," she said when her chin began to wobble.

She'd shed tears of anguish and joyful tears of love. All they'd done was cloud her vision. No more, she promised herself. Seeing Mark in action at the party had certainly eliminated the gray color Jared had talked about. No more!

Fear of losing Mark had distorted everything.

"Well, sweetheart," she muttered, "you can't lose something you've never had!"

CHAPTER ELEVEN

Mark thanked the electrical contractor who'd given him a lift back into St. Charles, then ran up the driveway. Noticing that her car wasn't in the garage, he charged up the back steps.

Where was she?

The house was ominously quiet.

"Sara!" he shouted. "Where are you?"

She should have been here by now, he thought, racing from one room to the other. He took the steps two at a time, calling her name frantically. He opened the bedroom door, taking a harsh breath before he walked in. "Sara?"

Fear lodging in his throat, he walked to the closet. Her clothes were there. He'd been scared to death that Linda had double-crossed him and told Sara the worst.

Where was she? He moved to the dresser and

opened the top drawer. He picked up a neatly folded lace-edged handkerchief. "Where is she?"

Hal said the last time he'd seen her was when he'd shown her where the ladies' room was. Martha wasn't any help. She'd given her husband a strange knowing look and walked toward the rose garden without speaking. Sara had simply vanished.

When he'd gone looking for the car, he knew something dreadful had happened. Sara wouldn't leave him stranded without a reason, a damn good reason. He'd run back to the house to find Linda. The flustered caterer told him that Linda had quit, right in the middle of serving the buffet.

A sinking sensation gnawed at the pit of his stomach as he imagined the absolute worst: Sara giving a talkative Linda a ride back into town.

He wrapped the corner of the flimsy piece of linen around his fingers. Flinging his arm over his eyes, he collapsed back onto the bed.

"Sara knows," he whispered fatalistically.

He racked his brain for a plausible explanation she would accept to excuse the multitude of lies he'd told her.

Silently cursing himself for lying to Sara to begin with, he wadded the handkerchief into the palm of his hand. Without Sara he'd be less than nothing. He'd fought the inevitable and lost.

The salty taste of defeat clogged his throat.

Sara entered the house, mentally preparing herself to pack her bags and leave before Mark returned. Explanations weren't necessary. He hadn't given any; why should she?

As though perceiving things through tunnel vision, she proceeded through the kitchen and hallway without seeing anything other than what was immediately in front of her. She'd only take her clothes. There were too many memories attached to Mark if she took anything else.

"Sara?" Mark sat up in the bed when she entered the room. With anxious eyes he scanned her face. She gave him one scathing glance, then moved to the closet and pulled the suitcases from the top shelf.

"You're leaving me, aren't you?" His voice cracked with fear.

"Yes."

"Because of the merger?"

"Partially."

"I'm the one who has to dance to Hal Moran's tune."

Sara unzipped the lid of the suitcase. She expressed her distaste with an unladylike snort. "Will money make you tone-deaf?" she asked sarcastically.

Sliding close to where she'd placed the suitcase on the bed, he clenched his hands to keep from physically stopping her quick movements. The look she'd given him reminded him of so many he'd received as a kid. It cut him to the quick.

"Would it make a difference if I told you I'd reconsidered? Manchester Homes will remain autonomous."

"No." She'd faced her biggest fear, his leaving, and made her decision. There was no going back.

"Why did you leave Moran's without me?"

"You were enjoying yourself. I wasn't. I left."

"Did someone offend you?"

"I found Hal Moran offensive, but you knew that before we went there." She speared him with a chilly glance. "Your behavior offended me."

"Kissing you in the rose garden?"

"Fondling the help," Sara blurted.

"What?"

"Are you wife-deaf as well as tone-deaf? I said—"

"I heard what you said. I didn't touch any other woman. Who told you I was 'fondling' the help?"

There was no mistaking the antagonism beaming from his dark eyes. His unctuous lies confirmed her suspicions. He could prevaricate with a straight face; not even his hands betrayed him.

"No one. I saw you."

Remembering the swish of taffeta across the front of his pants, his face turned crimson. "Is that why you're leaving?"

"Partially."

"I did *not* make a pass at Linda Turnball," he stated.

"Okay. I hallucinated the whole thing."

"Stop playing games, Sara. I swear—"

"Don't bother swearing," she interrupted, turning to empty the drawers.

"I love you, sweetheart. I'm not interested in any other woman. I can't handle the one I have."

For a fraction of a second Sara paused when

she heard his declaration of love. Glib lies, she silently protested.

Mark watched her stack the contents of the top drawer neatly into the suitcase. Her handkerchief in his hand was damp with perspiration. He couldn't give it to her any more than he could have returned the teacher's handkerchief with the bloodstain. He'd keep it, cherish it, because he knew that within the hour Sara would be out of his life unless he did something drastic.

"Did you talk to Linda?" he asked, twisting the cloth as though it were Linda's neck. "She told you about me, didn't she?"

"She didn't tell me anything I didn't already know."

Sara turned back to the dresser. In the mirror she saw Mark stiffen, then collapse backward.

"I knew I didn't have a chance once you found out the truth. I was a damn fool to think I could hide it from you."

As determined as she was to leave with a small scrap of her dignity, the utter despair in his voice brought tears to her eyes. The mirror reflected the pain etching his face. Small shudders rippled his chest. She watched his throat work convulsively, and tears cascaded from her eyes.

Without a doubt Mark would lie there on the bed as though strung on a rack, but he wouldn't budge an inch to stop her from leaving. Mark Manchester, the man she loved beyond reason, would never hold her close to his heart again. She would never touch those finely chiseled facial features, kiss the firm line of his lips until they gentled, stroke the dark lock of hair that fell forward, feel the hardness of his chest, share laughter, suffer the joy of bringing another child into the world. It would be over.

She merely had to zip up the suitcase and walk through the door.

Her shoulders sagged. Why? Why couldn't she? Why couldn't she propel herself through the door?

Mark raised his head. Burning blue eyes met velvet dark eyes. In a single moment their souls were bared.

"I don't want you to feel sorry for me. I'd hate that worse than having you despise me," Mark whispered hoarsely. "I don't want your pity."

"I'm the one to be pitied. I'm twenty-seven years old and feel eighty, close to death and not dreading it." She raised her eyes to the ceiling in an attempt to stop the flow of tears steadily tracking down her face. "Please, Mark, make me understand why you left me."

Mark sat on the edge of the bed, his hands woven together to give him the strength to answer. For so long he'd hidden what he was, who he was, that he wasn't sure he could explain. His lips moved, but no sound came from them.

Seeing him struggle, Sara crossed the room and knelt at his feet. "My pride kept me from saying how much I loved you the minute I ran up the steps of the house all sweaty and unkempt and found you here. I'm saying it now. With all my heart and soul I love you, Mark."

Mark scrutinized her face. No pity. No condem-

180

nation. Her eyes blazed with unconcealed love. He had to tell her, had to break through the foundation of lies that he'd built their marriage on, had to speak now or become an empty shell once she left him.

His throat worked. Lips dry, he muttered, "I was so scared you'd find out. I couldn't let you know that I'm a goddamn worthless bum. I knew you'd hate me when you did." He choked the damning phrases from their solid cage. "I screwed up. I didn't leave you, Sara—or Jamie." His shadowed eyes raised to the ceiling and he blinked rapidly. "Run, run, run! Pay the price. You can't have love without money!"

"I'd love you if we didn't have a dime," Sara whispered earnestly.

"My mom must have said that. She died at thirty-four, an old, brokenhearted woman. Drank herself to death when dad couldn't face not being able to support her and left." His knuckles turned white, his fingertips blue from the clamped pressure of his entwined hands. "Oh, Sara, I never realized . . . I did what he did! I hated him for being a coward and hated her for wallowing in self-pity. Oh, God, I'm worse than worthless. . . . I'm like them."

Sara slid between his knees. She pulled his head into the crook of her shoulder and neck. "Oh, my darling, you aren't worthless. You worked, provided for Jamie and me. Why didn't you tell me? It wouldn't have mattered."

"Wouldn't have mattered? You don't understand, Sara. I'm not talking about getting behind

181

on the bills. Gentile poverty? Hell, no, I'm from dirty, stinking poverty."

"I love you, Mark."

"You love a successful contractor who can keep you in a house that doesn't let the rain and the cold inside."

"I love you, not bricks and mortar," she reassured him, her fingers making small indentations as they dug into the fabric of his shirt. "I love the man who married me when he could have easily ignored me when I trapped him by getting pregnant."

"Don't you see, Sara? *I* trapped *you.* I'd been on the streets since I was nine. I knew how to prevent making babies. But I didn't protect you. After you told me I knew you'd marry me, or your parents would raise hell until you did. I did the trapping. Not intentionally," he amended, "not with malice or forethought, but I admit to silently giving a sigh of relief when you told me. I could be your devil and your savior rolled into one. Much better than the man I faced in the mirror every day."

He took a deep, weary breath. "But I loved you, Sara, since the day we met. I can remember that day as clearly as if it happened yesterday."

"I remember too. You were building the house next to my parents'. You came over to use the phone."

"I came over to meet you. I'd been watching you for days. I'd done everything I could think of to impress you, but you politely smiled when I said hello, then fled into your house. I knew I wasn't good enough for you to wipe your feet on, but—"

"But you showed a girl who'd been sheltered from experiencing anything firsthand how to leave books behind and live in the real world."

"Your dad should have followed his instincts and shot me before I dragged you down with me."

"Dragged me down? I was in heaven. You hung the moon and the stars, and everything in between," she argued. Those bright stars were captured in her dark eyes now. "Those first few months you convinced me I was your treasured angel."

"You were—are. You're everything I'm not. Everything I can never be. I learned early in life that you have to pay for everything. Charity is expensive."

"But not love," Sara protested.

Mark laughed without humor. "I remember Christmastime. Do you know what it's like to be poor then? Every night you go to bed with your stomach growling, but you dream. You dream about Santa Claus bringing you a sackful of toys. In first grade I remember listening to the older kids telling everybody there wasn't a Santa Claus. My God! No Santa Claus. No hope! Christmas morning I woke up before dawn and found a red paper sack with three packages inside. I cried. Cried like a damn baby. I'd been good. Santa hadn't forgotten me." His hand raised to the back of his neck and massaged it. "I paid for those three presents. That afternoon, the local newspaper had a photographer and writer at our house. They took my picture. The next morning, I quit my newspaper route. I couldn't bear for everyone to see my picture and know what a loser I was. A born loser. But I learned a lesson. You pay, one way or another, for everything."

Sara bowed her head. She'd seen similar pictures in the St. Charles paper at Christmastime. She'd felt compassion for those less fortunate than herself. Trying to be cruelly honest with herself, she delved into the past to see if she'd labeled the unfortunate children as losers. She hadn't.

"And that's why you bought all those gifts for Jamie and me?" Her throat closed with pain. Sara wished she could take back all the mean thoughts attached to each gift he'd given her. Those gifts had been expressions of love. Love the only way a deprived child who'd grown into a man could give it.

Mark nodded. "Expensive gifts . . . and you still didn't love me. You must have instinctively known all along how rotten I was."

A low groan of denial passed through Sara's lips. "I didn't understand. I thought you felt guilty about not loving me, having to marry me, and that's why you gave me the gifts."

"Sara, I've always loved you." His mouth twisted downward. "But I've always known that I'd destroy our marriage. When the economy slowed down and the interest rates rose, I knew I'd go bankrupt. I couldn't stand the thought of seeing failure written in your eyes or Jamie's. So I ran like a damn coward."

"Oh, God, Mark, what a mess we've made of things. Jamie loved you . . . with or without the gifts. He idolized you! I idolized you!"

"That's because you both didn't know that the man you idolized had his feet firmly planted in scum. I knew I'd screw up somewhere along the line."

"I hate hearing you degrade yourself." She leaned back, then tugged his hands away from each other. The wad of cloth fell to the carpet, unnoticed by Sara. "See these? They're you. Strong. Clean. Industrious. Independent." She framed her face with them. "I love your hands. I love how they make me feel when you're tender. Love their strength when they hold me as though I'm never close enough."

Mark rested his damp forehead against hers. Eyes closed, he listened but couldn't believe his good fortune. Only once had anyone other than Sara given him something for nothing. Blindly he lowered his hand and picked the handkerchief up from the floor.

"A long time ago a teacher bandaged my knee with her handkerchief. My blood stained it. I washed and washed it, but it wouldn't come clean. I'm like that limp piece of cloth. Stained. Believing that you and Jamie loved me was like believing in Santa Claus. You two were my hope. There were times when I almost convinced myself that you could love me."

"Almost?"

"Almost, but never really." His fingers dug into the palm of her hand. "If I were any kind of a man, I'd let you go."

"Don't I have any say in whether I go or stay?"

Silently Mark nodded. His stomach did a somersault when she rose to her feet. She'd spoken of feeling old; he felt ancient as he watched her feet move away from the bed.

For once in her life Sara knew exactly what she was doing: breaking the poverty cycle. She had to make Mark realize that he held his own fate in his capable hands.

"Where you were born, how you were raised, isn't important to me. To protect yourself you lied to me. The lies between us have to stop."

"How can I stop lying to you when I can't stop lying to myself?"

"By realizing what you are now—respected. Mark, people don't give a damn about your background." She paused. "*I* don't give a damn. Don't you see, Mark? You have to respect and love yourself or you'll never be able to love anyone else. You can't buy love!"

Mark threaded his fingers through the short hairs at his temple. He heard her. He wanted to believe her, but too many years of poverty and self-loathing threatened his reasoning.

"I love you, Mark, but I'm leaving you. I've fought for a lot of doomed causes. One of them was making you love me. I can't fight this battle for you. You've built everything but your own self-esteem. I can't do that for you."

"Don't leave," Mark whispered, willing to beg,

186

willing to grovel, knowing that he'd surely die without her.

"Think about it, Mark. What kind of man, or woman, for that matter, lets the person they love walk out of their lives without stopping them? Especially when they know that their love is returned. I let you go, but I was handicapped by fear. Fear that you didn't love me. Fear crippled me. Are you emotionally crippled, Mark? Or are you strong enough to stop me, stop the never-ending circle of fear that's destroying what we have?"

Mark groaned audibly, wiping his fingers on the crumpled handkerchief. "I can't stop you. Don't you see? You're better off without me. I'll only foul up again. It's part of my nature."

"Good-bye, Mark," Sara said, slowly walking through the door, giving him every chance to halt her progress.

Fourteen steps. Sara held her breath as she counted them before starting down. In less than fifteen seconds Mark had to decide whether or not the love she and Jamie had shown him proved his worthiness.

She gripped the banister, wondering if she'd asked too much, too soon. Sadly she shook her head. She'd meticulously avoided confrontations to guarantee their living together. Both of their doubts and fears had grown while she'd dithered. As much as she loved Mark, as much as she wanted him as a husband, she couldn't turn around and climb the four steps she'd descended.

The landing loomed in front of her. With each step her heart sank. Mark didn't love himself enough to love her. They had nothing to build their love on but heartache.

She wiped her eyes to keep the tears from blurring her vision.

She was on the bottom step when she heard him cry her name, then heard him pounding down the steps behind her. The earth seemed to shake beneath her feet. With one fell swoop he lifted her into his arms, crushing her against his chest.

"You aren't going anywhere without me, sweetheart." His voice was heavy with emotion. "I'm strong. As long as you love me, I can be anything I want to be."

For long, silent moments they held each other, as though by holding on tight they'd never separate again.

Finally a shy smile teased Sara's lips. She whispered, "And can I be what I want to be?"

"Mmm." He carried her up the steps two at a time. "Anything in particular other than Mrs. Sara Manchester?"

"A mother."

Mark stopped in his tracks, grinning from ear to ear. "Would you mind repeating yourself?"

"I want children, your children. Plural."

"Plural?" A small frown pleated his brow for a second. "You hated being pregnant. Morning sickness, dizziness, expanding waistline. You don't have to prove you love me by having my child." He carefully placed her in the center of the bed.

"Say what you mean, Mark. Does the thought of having a child make you sick?"

"There can't be another Jamie. He was . . . special."

"Jamie was a love child, but I'm capable of loving any child that's a bit of you and a bit of me. Remember Jamie's last birthday wish?"

Mark slowly fumbled with the buttons down the front of her jumpsuit. "Twins. A brother and a sister."

"It's possible, you know. My great-aunts were twins."

She'd been denied the pleasure of planning a baby the first time. Uncertain that Mark wanted a child, she'd kept her thoughts to herself. Silly thoughts like what color hair and eyes the child would have, who it would look like, and whether it would be a boy or a girl—or even twins.

"Do you think . . ." Mark felt foolish when he realized the question on the tip of his tongue.

Without secrets and fears between them Sara knew what he was about to ask. "I know there's a heaven. I think he will." She added positively, "I'm sure Jamie will know."

Mark's blue eyes shone brightly with what she suspected were tears. His tears and his tenderness and his touch told her that he would always be with her, as close as two souls touching. His tears of love cleansed those of anguish.

Now you can reserve July's Candlelights before they're published!

♥ You'll have copies set aside for *you*
   the instant they come off press.

♥ You'll save yourself precious shopping
   time by arranging for *home delivery.*

♥ You'll feel proud and efficient about
   organizing a system that *guarantees* delivery.

♥ You'll avoid the disappointment of not
   finding *every* title you want and need.

ECSTASY SUPREMES $2.75 each

☐ 129 **SHADOWS OF THE HEART**, Linda Vail 17794-4-13
☐ 130 **CONTINENTAL LOVER**, Cathie Linz 11440-3-48
☐ 131 **A MAN FOR AMY**, Blair Cameron 15314-X-18
☐ 132 **A FORBIDDEN REFUGE**, Eleanor Woods 12733-5-26

ECSTASY ROMANCES $2.25 each

☐ 442 **FEVER PITCH**, Pamela Toth 12505-7-30
☐ 443 **ONE LOVE FOREVER**, Christine King 16608-X-11
☐ 444 **WHEN LIGHTNING STRIKES**, Lori Copeland 19420-2-29
☐ 445 **WITH A LITTLE LOVE**, Natalie Stone 19546-2-10
☐ 446 **MORNING GLORY**, Donna Kimel Vitek 15567-8-12
☐ 447 **TAKE CHARGE LADY**, Alison Tyler 18478-9-22
☐ 448 **ISLAND OF ILLUSIONS**, Jackie Black 14147-8-14
☐ 449 **THE PASSIONATE SOLUTION**, Jean Hager 16777-9-32